BOOK 2

TROY ANDREWS
AND THE
JUNIOR DEPUTIES

THE
MAN WITH THE
TERRIBLE
SECRET

Richard

BOOK 2

TOBY ANDREWS AND THE JUNIOR DEPUTIES

THE MAN WITH THE TERRIBLE SECRET

JERRY B. JENKINS

Author of The Dallas O'Neill Mystery Series

MOODY PRESS
CHICAGO

ISBN: 0-8024-1626-8

1 3 5 7 9 10 8 6 4 2

Printed in the United States of America

To the last sixth-grade class
at Waukegan Christian School

Contents

Thomas's Story

How could I have known the first time I met Max Carney at the Lake Farm Home that he would become the center of a mystery I would never forget? He seemed like any other adult at the time. I didn't know he had any secrets, let alone one that I would eventually reveal.

If it wasn't for my friendship with Thomas Christian, I probably never would have met Mr. Carney. Thomas lived at Lake Farm, where Mr. Carney was a night supervisor.

The other four Kalamazoo County Junior Deputies (not counting my little sister, Kate) were my best friends, but if I had to choose a favorite, a *best* best friend, it would have been Thomas. We were the same age and in the same grade (though not in the same room), but Thomas looked older by at least two years. In fact, a lot of people thought he was even older than that. He was only twelve, but he looked old enough to drive a car.

He already had muscles and sideburns and even hair on his legs. Thomas was tall and dark with curly black hair. His face didn't have that baby-fat look so many of my friends and I still had.

Thomas was as tough as he looked, or at least he was fearless. I hardly ever saw him fight, because no one had the courage to mess with him. He could have fun and laugh, but most of the time he looked pretty serious. That was the only thing that bothered me about him.

It wasn't Thomas's fault, of course. He didn't have parents. At least he didn't know where they were. He lived with a couple of hundred other kids at the Lake Farm Boys and Girls Home on Oakland Drive. Around our school they were known as the Lake Farmers.

Mostly the Lake Farmers stuck together. They didn't have many friends outside their own group. Their clothes were plain, and they all wore the same military-style coats in the winter—navy pea coats. They caused most of the trouble and did most of the fighting at our school. If a so-called "normal" kid had a friend who was a Lake Farmer, it was usually because he needed a tough bodyguard.

I didn't need a bodyguard. That wasn't why Thomas was my friend. We just got along and slowly got to know each other. Anyway, my parents always told me that people are people. We shouldn't label them as orphans or people of different colors or backgrounds. We should judge them by how they act and what they say. That's one reason the Junior Deputies also included a younger boy, my little sister, a black kid, and a freckle-faced redhead. In order, they were Joel McBride, who was only ten; Kate, who was only eight; Daniel Jackson; and Jonathan Bynum. The only thing we had in common was that we all went to the same church.

Daniel, the black kid, loved to say, "If God is your Father, that makes me your brother." Then he'd imitate his dad, a huge man with a deep voice, and say, "Deal with it!"

Daniel was one of very few people who could get a laugh out of Thomas. Most of the time Old Tom, as I liked to call him, was serious. Whenever he came with us to church or spent time at my house, my parents had to sign him out of the Lake Farm Home and agree to be his guardians for however long he was gone. I think, at times like that, he pretended we were his family.

One Sunday afternoon after dinner, about a half hour before my dad drove Thomas back, Mom asked if I could ever visit him at the Home. I tried to catch her eye and shake my head, but she wasn't looking.

Thomas was silent for a long time. "I don't think that would be such a good idea," he said.

But Mom kept at it. "Do they allow it? Can kids come and spend a night and join in the activities?"

Thomas pressed his lips together and shook his head. "They can visit, but they can't stay over."

"Well, maybe just a few hours then," Mom said.

"I don't think Toby would like it," Thomas said suddenly. He had told me that before. "It's more like prison than a home."

Mom laughed. "Oh, surely not, Thomas. What do you mean?"

"We all have to line up in teams and count off, and we eat the same slop all the time."

Mom tried to excuse the Home, saying that they probably had to buy their food in large quantities to save money.

It was obvious Thomas didn't want to talk anymore about where he lived.

I had always been curious about the place. Whenever we picked him up or dropped him off, it was at the main entrance in a big office building. I could see the open area where the kids played and the dormitories in the distance. One time Thomas pointed out the dining hall. But I had never been inside those buildings. Whenever I brought up the idea, he changed the subject or just said I wouldn't like it.

Something about living in a home like that with a bunch

of other kids seemed kind of cool to me. Not that I would ever want to leave my family or have to live like that. One thing I couldn't figure out, though, was why the place was named Lake Farm. There was no lake, and I didn't see anything like a farm either. I mean, there were gardens, but no fields, no tractors, no animals.

Thomas and I sat in the backseat of our station wagon when Dad drove him to and from Lake Farm. It was at times like that that I felt lucky. Hardly anyone else could get Thomas to talk, but for some reason he talked to me whenever no one else could hear us.

It had been during a ride in the car—one Sunday when my dad had gotten permission to take Thomas with us on a drive into Indiana—that Thomas told me how he had come to Lake Farm four years before.

He didn't look at me when he talked. Kate was in the backseat that day, so Thomas and I were jammed into the cargo area of the station wagon. We were too close to be looking at each other, so Thomas could just look out the window as he talked, and I was the only one in the car who could hear him. I could see his face only when passing cars made him reflect in the window.

"I was just starting second grade," he said, "and my aunt was getting married. She's the one who gave me the news."

"The news?" I said.

"That I couldn't live with her anymore."

"Why were you living with her in the first place?" I wanted to ask why he didn't live with his mom and dad, but my mother had told me not to ask a question like that. She said he would tell me himself if he wanted. She said that it was too personal, maybe too painful, and certainly none of my business unless he made it my business.

"I never knew my dad," he said quietly. "My aunt told me he and my mom never got married. He just took off and never saw me. My mom was still in high school when she had me, and somehow my aunt got stuck with me." Thomas was silent, then he chuckled. "Ooh, my aunt would be mad if she heard me say that."

"Why?"

"She never let me get away with saying stuff like that. She said she wasn't stuck with me but that God gave me to her. She said I was her assignment from Him, just the same way I get homework assignments at school. I'm just glad she took care of me better than I do my homework!"

I laughed. "My dad says you have street smarts, though," I said. "Even if you're not a great student."

"He said that?"

I nodded.

"Well, he ought to know. A deputy sheriff must run into all kinds of people who are street smart. So what he's saying is that I'd be a better criminal than a student."

I started to argue, but Thomas told me he was just kidding. "Anyway, your dad is right. Lake Farmers have to have street smarts, or we'd never survive."

"Why?"

"Well, most of us show up the same way I did. Nobody can take care of you anymore, your parents aren't around, and everybody thinks you would be better off in a Home somewhere."

"Why couldn't your aunt take care of you anymore?"

"Like I said, she was getting married. That was a bad day when she told me. I was pretty mad for a long time. I knew the guy she was marrying, and I liked him. I never talked about it, but I had been secretly hoping and praying that nothing would change. I figured he'd become my uncle. 'Course, he did become my uncle, but I never lived with my aunt after the wedding. When they left for their honeymoon, I was brought to Lake Farm."

"Do you mind if I ask why?"

Thomas shrugged but didn't answer right away. I could

13

see what Mom meant about this being none of my business and maybe not easy to talk about. But he finally told me. It was dark outside, and Kate was sleeping. Dad was driving back toward Kalamazoo County after our day at the Indiana sand dunes.

"My aunt and her fiancé had been going out together for about six months. I had babysitters more than ever, but that was all right. I had been with my aunt for so long, she was like my mother. She treated me like I was hers, anyway, except I never called her Mom. She had always told me I was her nephew and that my mother—her sister—loved me but had a lot of problems. Even back then my aunt told me I should respect my mom for doing the right thing and letting someone else raise me."

"What did you think about that?"

"I didn't know what to think. I'd been with my aunt since I was a baby, so I never knew anything or anybody else. Everybody else I knew had a mom and called her Mom. The woman raising me was my aunt, and that was all right with me. I saw pictures of my mom, who looked a lot like my aunt, and one time she visited me."

"She did?" I had been dying to ask if Thomas had ever met or even seen his real mom, but I knew I shouldn't.

Thomas nodded. "My aunt made a big deal about it for a couple of weeks. I think I was six, so I didn't know what to think. My real mother was coming to visit. I said something like, 'I don't have to leave and go with her, do I?' My aunt told me of course not, and after a while her excitement started rubbing off on me."

"You really wanted to meet your mom?"

"Yeah, but I didn't know what to expect."

"You weren't mad at her for not keeping you?"

"Like I am now, you mean?"

I wasn't sure that's what I meant, but I nodded anyway.

"No. I wasn't mad at her. All I knew was, she was my real

14

mom and she had left me with my aunt to raise me. My aunt was so excited about her visit that I figured it must be a big deal."

"Was it?"

"It was when she didn't show up. That's when my aunt said too much, and I got an idea what the real story was. She had me all cleaned up and dressed nice. I had Sunday shoes on, my hair combed, and all that. I couldn't have friends over, and I couldn't play outside. My mother was supposed to come over at two o'clock."

"But she didn't?"

"Not at two. I'd been playing on the living room floor while my aunt cleaned up the house. It looked as shiny as I did. Finally, just before two she went and changed her clothes, then came out and tucked my shirt in, combed my hair again, put my toys away, and had me sit right in the middle of the couch, facing the door. She asked me if I wasn't excited, so I just nodded. How was I supposed to know how to react?"

"So your mother never showed up?"

"Not when she was supposed to. My aunt kept looking at her watch and telling me to sit still. She was making me nervous, pacing, looking out the window, talking to herself. I kept begging to at least play on the floor again. Finally she said, 'Go ahead, what do I care?' and she started muttering about her sister being a bum, irresponsible, and all that."

"What did you think?"

"I just wished my mother wasn't coming. I didn't know her, didn't need to see her. I was curious about her, but it wasn't worth all that. I didn't like seeing my aunt all upset. At about three o'clock she let me change into my jeans and play outside. 'Get as dirty as you want,' she said. 'I don't much care what you look like when and if she ever gets here.'"

"When did she finally show up?"

"That evening, about an hour before I was supposed to go

to bed. She apologized to my aunt and said she had gotten hung up. That's when my aunt really exploded. She said, 'Yeah, well, I've been hung up for years since you disappeared from his life. Is it too much to ask that you be responsible for one afternoon?'

"They argued in front of me for a while, then my mother knelt and looked close at me. She said, 'He looks like his dad, doesn't he?'

"'How would I know?' my aunt said."

"What did you think of your mother?"

"Well, she looked a lot older than the picture my aunt kept of her. She dressed kind of sloppy and wild, and my aunt kept making her go outside to smoke. She didn't talk to me much, and I finally realized that she wasn't there because she wanted to be. She was there because somebody talked her into it. I was as glad as she was when she finally left.

"I never saw her or heard from her again."

The Home

Ifelt bold enough to ask Thomas why he couldn't still live with his aunt after she married. When he reacted by sitting very still and staring out the car window without speaking, I decided my mother had been right. I had asked the wrong thing, had brought up a painful subject.

But I guess it wasn't that Thomas didn't want to talk about it. He wanted to think about how he was going to say it, because he wanted me to understand.

"When I think back about it," he said, "I should have seen it coming. One day my aunt told me that she and her boyfriend were getting married. She didn't say anything about me now having a man in the house, and I didn't ask.

"But a few weeks later I heard her talking about their new house—some place they were renting that was closer to his work. All that talk about moving, and I never once asked about my room, where I would stay, anything like that."

"You must have wondered," I said.

"I really didn't. I didn't worry about stuff like that. I was the only kid I knew who was being raised by his aunt, but lots of kids had divorced parents, and the kids lived with one for a while and then the other. I was a pretty happy kid and didn't worry about what would happen to me. I figured we'd have a wedding, we'd move, they'd show me where my bed was, and that would be that."

"So you didn't know anything until the day of the wedding?"

"Oh, yeah, she told me before I was taken to Lake Farm. But not much before. I think she wanted to. She kept saying we had to talk about some serious things, but it just didn't hit me. I guess I should have known, but what does a kid know? I trusted everybody then."

"Do you trust anybody now?"

Thomas nodded. "I trust you and your mom and dad. I trust the other guys. My aunt was a good person. Now that I think about it, she didn't *have* to raise me for those first few years. She says it was her duty to see that I became a Christian. And maybe she never promised that I would be with her forever, but I sure never had a reason to think I wouldn't."

"How did she tell you?"

"She put it off a long time—I remember that. She got more and more busy with the wedding and the move, and it started to sink in that she never talked about me helping with the packing and the moving. Finally I asked her if I could help the guys carry furniture when moving day came. She said we'd have to talk about that. I still didn't get it."

"When did she finally tell you?"

"The day before the wedding. She had a long talk with her boyfriend, and then he left. She got all dressed up for the rehearsal and got me fitted with a suit so I could be a junior groomsman. Then she told me to sit in the living room so she could talk to me. When she sat me in the middle of the couch, the same place I had waited for my mother, I knew something was up.

"She started crying even before she started talking. I hadn't seen her cry that much. She was a pretty happy person. That scared me, but I listened. She said she had come to a very difficult decision, the hardest decision she had ever made since the day she had agreed to take me in.

" 'It's not fair to my new husband to expect him to raise you,' she said. 'He thinks you're great, of course, but we're going to want to start our own family, and you're not really his responsibility.'

"I guess I wasn't her responsibility either, but that hadn't stopped her from raising me for almost seven years already. But pretty soon I knew what was coming. I thought at first she was going to make me live with her parents—my grandparents. But both of them were alcoholics, I think. My aunt was the only Christian in the family."

"Was she marrying a Christian?"

"Yeah. She met him at our church."

"Then why wouldn't he take you in?"

Thomas shrugged and bit his lip. "I don't know. I couldn't argue with her or with him. I'd never had a say in what happened to me. Everything had been fine up until then, except when we went to family picnics and stuff and my grandparents started yelling at each other. I told my aunt, 'I'm not staying with Grandma and Grandpa!'

"She said, 'Oh, I'd never make you do that. I found a place that has lots of kids of all ages and lots of things to do.'

"I didn't want to hear it. I wanted to shout and scream and cry and beg her to not send me away, but what could I do? She told me she loved me and hated to do it, but she had to think of herself and her new husband. What I didn't get was why keeping me would be so bad for them. It had to be his problem, you know, because I think it was really hard on her to let me go.

"She said it was a money thing too. The government or somebody pays for me to stay at Lake Farm. Nobody had

19

given her any money for me up to then, not even my own mother."

"Did you cry?"

"I wanted to. I was too stunned. And then, when I finally thought I might cry, I decided not to. I figured that if they didn't want me, I didn't want them. I was scared to death and felt unwanted. She kept telling me that it wasn't that she didn't love me and want me and it wasn't that she wouldn't miss me terribly. But after a while I realized that she was talking to herself, not to me.

"There was no other way to take it. My mother had never wanted me. My grandparents sure couldn't take me in, thank goodness. And now my aunt—the only mother I had ever known—was sending me away. The only thing I asked her was, 'How long will I be there?'

"When she looked down before she answered, I knew I was never coming back. She said she would visit me as much as she could, but that's been only like once a year, because they don't have a lot of money and they're over six hundred miles away."

"What did she do?" I asked. "Put you on a train?"

Thomas shook his head. "She packed up my stuff, told me I could keep the wedding suit, and introduced me to her uncle, an old guy who lives in Flint. She said he would be driving me to Kalamazoo to drop me off at Lake Farm."

"Did you know this guy?"

"I'd seen him a couple of times, but I don't think I had ever talked to him. That was a weird day. I stood there in the wedding, trying to keep from crying. My aunt and I had already said good-bye, and she hugged me real tight. They had the reception, and then she and her husband ran out to their car, and we threw rice at them. Then that old great-uncle of mine told me he thought we'd better hit the road."

"Was he creepy?"

"Not really. He just didn't know how to talk to a kid, and I sure wasn't in any talking mood. He bought me some food and kept asking if I was all right. I didn't say much, so he finally gave up. I'll bet we didn't say two words for the last three hours of the trip. We pulled into the driveway after dark. Finally he said, 'You're going to be all right. This is the best place for you.'

"He helped carry my stuff inside, gave an envelope from my aunt to the night man, Mr. Carney, and signed a paper. Then he reached out to shake my hand. I didn't want to shake his hand. What did that mean? I couldn't refuse though, so I took it, but not tight enough.

"He said, 'C'mon, little man. Give me a grip. You're gonna hafta be a man in here.' He smiled, but I couldn't. I gripped tighter, and he held me close. I could feel his wool sweater and smell his aftershave lotion. 'You might have to beat up a few guys in here,' he said. 'Can you do that?'

"I shook my head. I had never fought anyone. 'There's no science to it,' he said. 'They'll test you. Make sure you hit first and hit hard. They'll leave you alone after that.'

"I didn't say anything. Mr. Carney said, 'Sir, we're not big on long good-byes here.' And my great-uncle said, 'We hardly know each other. I'm leaving.' He turned back to me and said, 'Take care of yourself.' And that was it. I wouldn't have even known the word then, but all of a sudden, I was an orphan. A Lake Farmer."

"And was he right? Did the kids test you?"

Thomas smiled and nodded. "They sure did. Even though Mr. Carney said they wouldn't. He told me they kept the boys and girls separate and that they also kept the older boys and the younger boys separate. For some reason the older boys never hassled the younger ones. I guess there was some kind of a code that made you look like a sissy if you picked on the younger kids. But there was enough fighting among the kids in the same age groups anyway. There were always big fights in the older boys' dorms. In ours the fights were usually one against one."

"Did you have to fight?"

"Are you kidding? I was tested that first night. Like I said, I had never fought before. But my great-uncle's advice came in handy."

"What happened?"

"Well, it was pretty late, long after lights out, so Mr. Carney didn't spend a lot of time talking to me. He just told me a few rules, told me where the bathrooms were and what to do in the morning to find the dining hall. Then he walked me over to the dorm, introduced me to the dorm counselor, and they helped me slide my stuff under my bed. I was in a room that had thirty bunk beds in it, where the elementary kids slept. I thought everybody was asleep."

"They weren't?"

"Nope. They all knew somebody new was coming, the same way we know it now. As soon as Mr. Carney left and the dorm counselor went back to bed in a little room at one end, I sat on the edge of the bed and got undressed. It was the first time I hadn't prayed before bed that I could remember, but I was mad at God. I felt like He had left me alone. I hated everything and everybody, and I wanted to die. I didn't care what happened to me.

"As soon as I got under the covers of a bottom bunk, I heard guys tiptoeing over. They started whispering, asking me my name, where I was from, all that. Then I realized they didn't care. They were just distracting me so someone else could start going through my stuff. There wasn't much there, for sure nothing worth stealing, but I felt movement under the bed."

"What did you do?"

"I thought of what my uncle had said, and even though no one was fighting me, I figured this was a test. The guys I was mad at were the ones under the bed, but I knew the ones

22

talking to me in the dark were just as guilty. I was scared and lonely and sad, but mostly I was so mad I couldn't stand it. I never gave a second thought to what kind of trouble I might get into. I just decided to hit first and hit hard."

"Who'd you hit?"

"I didn't know until the next morning when I saw one guy with a swollen eye and another with a fat lip. I knew they couldn't see me in the dark, and all I could see of them was just their outlines against the hall light. I had never hit anybody before, but all my anger boiled over at once. I don't even know who I was maddest at—probably my aunt because she claimed to love me but sent me away.

"I threw the first punch so fast and so straight and hard that I felt my fist smack against someone's forehead. He flopped right over on his back and hit the floor. The one sitting on my bed turned to run, and I socked him in the mouth as he turned away. Just the sound of those two punches sent all those guys scrambling out of there.

"The dorm counselor came out and asked what was going on, but everybody was back in bed, and no one was saying anything. He said, 'Hey, new kid, Thomas Christian, what are you doin' out of bed?'

"'Some of my stuff fell out of my suitcase,' I told him. He said, 'Leave it till morning,' but I didn't care. He didn't stay around to see if I left it or not, so I put everything away and got back into bed. Then I said, just loud enough for the guys to hear, 'I don't care who I hurt, so if anybody wants any more, bring it on.' "

"You said that?"

Thomas nodded. "I don't even know how I thought of it. It wasn't that I was so tough or brave. I was scared to death, but I didn't care anymore. I wouldn't have cared if ten guys had jumped me. I'd have hurt as many of them as I could, and then I would have been glad if they'd beat the tar out of me. I was in a rage for months, and I didn't care."

Max Carney

The first time I had ever heard of Max Carney was in Thomas's story about his first night at Lake Farm. His name hardly made a dent in my brain then. Thomas told me lots more stories about Lake Farm and how he got his reputation as a tough kid, even though he wasn't so big when he got there.

Somehow the word got around that he was not someone to mess with. He never told anyone that he had never fought before, but he was looked upon with awe because the two kids he had smacked in the face were older and considered tough guys. When Thomas saw them in the light of day, he was surprised. They were impressed that he hadn't told on them the night before.

"I still wasn't afraid to fight them. I would fight anybody. Down deep I wanted to run, to cry, to hide under covers and sleep my life away. I didn't know what to do with my anger. There was no one to talk to. Kids who came and cried were treated bad, laughed at, called sissies, and usually wound up being shipped somewhere else. I had no idea where that might be, so I just became tough."

"Weren't you scared?"

"Sure, but who was I going to tell? The day and night supervisors were nice enough, but they didn't care. They had jobs to do. None of them, not even the counselors, got actually close to any of us. We had our favorites, people we liked, but usually they were college kids who went back to school. I didn't dare try to get close to anybody, because I knew they would be gone."

"Weren't there any workers who stayed for years?"

"Sure, but they must have kept themselves from getting too close to the kids because the *kids* eventually left. You didn't dare get too honest with anybody. The thing was, though, I could see myself in everybody else. We were all acting the same way, and I'll bet we all thought we were the only ones pretending to be tough. I felt like a phony for years—and the more I felt that way, the more I tried to be tough. It was amazing how little I ever had to fight, because everybody could just tell I didn't care whether I got hurt or lived or died."

"Did your aunt visit you?"

"About once a year, like I said. She looked shocked at how I had grown and how I didn't look like an innocent little boy anymore. She smiled at me and hugged me, but I didn't smile or hug her back until the last visit, after I had been going to church with you guys for a while."

"Did her husband come with her?"

"No. They always used the excuse that he was working, but I told her I didn't want to see him. I didn't say why, but she knew. I knew it was his fault I wasn't living with her anymore. I blamed her too, of course. She chose him over me. What she did makes sense now that I understand a little more, but I still think she could have kept me. I'm working on it, but I'm still mad at her for that."

26

"Who's your favorite worker at Lake Farm?"

"I liked Buzz Griffin, who worked last summer. He goes to a Christian college in the Upper Peninsula, and he started a Bible club for the Christian kids. I don't know how he got permission, and it wasn't something official from Lake Farm. You could come to it if you wanted, during playtime after dinner each night."

"How many came?"

"Not many. Nobody wanted to give up that time. There were about nine of us."

"Bet you miss him."

Thomas nodded.

"You told me once you liked Mr. Carney at first."

"Sort of. Only because he's never mean. But he's not that nice either. He's just there. He makes sure we follow all the rules, and he never cuts anybody any slack. If you do everything you're supposed to, he leaves you alone. If you get into trouble, he makes sure you pay."

"Is he the one who's always standing in the window, staring out when we take you back on Sundays?"

"That's him."

"He doesn't look so scary."

"He's not. He just never smiles. He works Sunday afternoons and then all the nights until Friday. Then we don't see him again from early Friday morning until Sunday afternoon."

"How long has he been working there?"

"Forever. Since long before I got there. Somebody said they thought he'd been there twenty years. He lives over by the park."

"Where's that?"

"Down by Oakwood Beach, not far from Park View."

"My cousin has a paper route down in there," I said. "I help him with it sometimes. I wonder if I've ever delivered to his house."

"Probably."

That night, when we finally got back to Lake Farm to drop off Thomas, sure enough, Mr. Carney was standing in the window, peering out.

"Isn't that nice," my mother said. "He's watching for you."

"More likely he's going to bawl you out because I'm late."

"Oh, we're not late, are we?" Mom said. "Phil, you told him eleven, didn't you?"

"That's what I put on the card I signed," my dad said. "'Course it *is* almost ten after."

"Surely he's not going to quibble about ten minutes," Mom said. "Certainly he'll just be glad to have Thomas back in one piece."

Thomas laughed. "Yeah, that's likely. This place can't get along without me."

"I'll sign you back in," Dad said.

"Phil, take Toby in there with you, so Mr. Carney can get a look at him, and ask him about Toby visiting for a meal one of these days."

"Oh, Mom!" I said. It wasn't really something I wanted to do.

Thomas made a face too, but there's no arguing with Mom when she gets one of these ideas.

"C'mon, boys," Dad said.

Mom waited in the car with the sleeping Kate.

Thomas and I stretched and sucked in the cold night air.

Mr. Carney was not in a good mood. He wasn't mean or anything, just cold and formal. "You're late, Mr. Christian," he said softly as we entered.

"And good evening to you, sir," my dad said. "Correction. Thomas is not late. *I* am late. I have responsibility for him, and I should have had him here—what?—nine minutes ago."

"Point taken," Mr. Carney said, not looking up or smiling.

"I would appreciate a call when you're going to be late."

"Even just a few minutes?" Dad asked.

"Even one minute," Mr. Carney said, opening a three-ring binder with policies and rules in it. He shoved it across the desk to my dad.

We all leaned in to see that residents were expected back in precisely when they were promised.

"My fault," Dad said.

"We've been through that," Mr. Carney said. He still wasn't being ugly, but why did he have to be so stiff and cold?

Dad signed the card that said he had brought Thomas back, just as he did every Sunday afternoon following church and dinner at our house. "If you will forgive me, sir," Dad said, "I was wondering if it would ever be possible to have my son visit Thomas here occasionally."

"We have visitors all the time," Mr. Carney said. "Not overnight, but there are opportunities."

"Such as?"

"From after school through dinner. That would be from about four to precisely seven."

"And how do we arrange that?"

"Through me. When would you like to do that?"

"Tomorrow?" Thomas suggested.

"Let's not do too much at once," Dad said. "How about Wednesday?"

Mr. Carney logged it in his book, but still there was no smile, no "We'll see you then" or "We're looking forward to it." He just closed the book and asked Thomas if he wished to be accompanied to his dorm.

"Nope. Not afraid of the dark anymore. Anyway, I know the counselor calls you to tell you I made it in all right."

Dad and I smiled. Thomas wasn't funny very often, but when he was, he made us laugh.

But not Mr. Carney. "Indeed," he said. Not a fun guy.

"See you in school tomorrow," I said.

"Yeah."

"And I'll see you when we come to pick up Toby Wednesday night," Dad said. "I assume it's all right that he comes directly here with you after school."

Thomas started to answer, but Mr. Carney softly interrupted. "Are you asking him or me?"

"I really don't care where the answer comes from," my dad said, and I could tell he was starting to get irritated with Mr. Carney. "As long as I get the information."

"Then you'll want the answer from me," Mr. Carney said. "Yes, your son—" and he paused to look down at his log "— Toby, may come directly here from school. You will be expected to pick him up at seven."

"Got it."

"Not seven-oh-five or seven-oh-nine."

"I said I got it," Dad snapped, and he looked as if he was going to really give it to Mr. Carney. But he caught himself. He had taken a police training course about dealing with ornery people, and he had learned to save his anger for when he really needed it.

On Wednesday, I walked with Thomas and fifty or sixty other Lake Farmers from my school to the Home. I was surprised to hear the names they were called, the taunts they had to listen to.

"Is it this way every day?" I asked.

Thomas nodded. "Of course, nobody ever says this stuff to one of us when we're alone, or when they're alone. And nobody calls me names directly."

"You never get in trouble for fighting at school?"

"I don't have to fight anymore. You get a reputation, you can live on that for a long time. Anyway, I fought a kid in fourth grade—"

"I remember that."

"And he told on me, so I beat him up again."

"You got in big trouble for that."

"Yeah, I did. But it was almost worth it. I never had any trouble with him again. I started feeling bad about it, because I knew I wasn't supposed to do that as a Christian. But I wondered how much God would want me to take. Even Jesus got mad and kicked people out of the temple. But I decided He wasn't defending Himself. He was sticking up for God. I haven't beat on anybody for a couple of years, but I sure don't want anybody to think I wouldn't if I had to."

The first hour and a half after school was homework time for the Lake Farmers. I decided I might as well do mine too. The kids all sat in long rows in a big room, and they weren't allowed to talk, except to ask for help from the leaders.

I guess I was looking sort of bored when Mr. Carney came by and whispered, "No one promised this would be fun."

"It's fun enough," I said. "Can we go when Thomas is finished with his homework?"

"You could, but Thomas never finishes his homework. If he did, he would get better grades, wouldn't you, Thomas?"

Thomas just pursed his lips and nodded.

"He'll be limited, as usual, to forty-five minutes playtime before getting ready for dinner. Then, after you leave, he'll get another hour and a half of free time."

The only thing we could do in the short time between homework and dinner was to play some tetherball and a little softball. It was fun, and I always liked being with my best friend, but it was hard not to be sad too. I could see in the faces of the kids, especially the younger ones, exactly what Thomas had told me about. They were afraid. They were mad. They had been left here, and yet they couldn't cry about it. If they did, they would be called sissies, and it would be worse.

When my dad came to get me and I signed out, I asked

Mr. Carney if it was true he lived near Oakwood Beach.

"Who told you that?" he said. "Thomas? How would he know?"

I didn't say. "Is it a secret?"

"From these kids, yes. I don't need them knowing where I live. I've had enough pranks pulled over the years."

"I've probably delivered your paper a few times," I said, trying to change the subject. "Sometimes I help my cousin on his route down there. You get the *Gazette?*"

He nodded.

"His name's Wayne. Know him?"

He shook his head. "My wife handles all that stuff."

Both Dad and I said good-bye to him as we left, but he said nothing. He didn't even look up from his paperwork.

I couldn't figure him out. He wasn't nasty or loud. He was just snotty. It's too bad he couldn't enjoy working with kids. That seemed like a fun job, and I thought it would be neat if there was someone at a place like Lake Farm who really loved the kids, and it showed.

I didn't care if I ever saw Mr. Carney again. I had no idea I'd see him again soon—and certainly not where I expected.

Bike Camp

Over spring break my parents sent me to a Christian bike camp in Muskegon, Michigan, several hours from our home. When I first heard about it, I was not excited. Then I found out that Daniel Jackson and Jonathan Bynum were going. It would have been great to have had little Joel McBride and Thomas Christian with us too, but Joel was too young, and the camp was too expensive for Thomas.

It was a pretty neat idea. This was a normal Christian camp, just like others I had been to, with one major difference. Each camper had to bring his own bike and be prepared to ride several hours a day. Campers were separated into teams, and each team stayed in its own cabin. The cabins were about a mile from the central meeting room and the dining hall, so we would be expected to ride our bikes just about everywhere we went.

There would also be obstacle courses, races, scavenger hunts, map and compass trips, and even stunt training for those who had bikes that could take it. I'm afraid Big Dan and Red Jon and I talked so much about the upcoming camp that Thomas and Joel were jealous.

"I don't care if I am two years younger," Joel said. "I can still outride any of you."

We all laughed and teased him, saying he was bragging and wrong besides. The truth was, he was almost right. He couldn't outride Thomas, of course, but a lot of times he *was* first in our bike races. He had a small stunt bike and could do all kinds of things we couldn't do. He was miserable about not going and was already looking forward to next year.

"We'll all be too old by then," I told him. "You'll be there on your own."

"You guys are no competition anyway," he said. "It would be too embarrassing for you if your little friend made you look bad."

Jonathan smiled that goofy smile of his and shook his head, his red hair flopping. For once he was speechless.

Big Dan's eyes were dancing. "I'm gonna smuggle you there to be my assistant," he said. "You can carry stuff for me and work on my bike. Change flat tires and all that."

Kate insisted that she wanted no part of a stupid bike camp. I think she really wanted to go.

Thomas was the most disappointed, though he didn't say much in front of the others. At Sunday dinner he told me he was going to start saving his money so he could go next year. "They *do* have bike camps for when you're thirteen, right?" he said.

I nodded.

"If I skip buying candy at the canteen every week," he added, "I'll have enough."

I wished we could pay his way so he could go this year, but my dad explained to me that with our new house and all the expenses of my big brother's illness—Jason had died several months before—we really didn't have a lot of extra money.

"Anyway," Dad said, "it will be a good experience for Thomas to save and sacrifice for something he wants. He'll appreciate it more. You know, Toby, those Lake Farm kids are often made to feel like charity cases. They get a lot of stuff given to them by generous people. That's good and necessary. But you can imagine how they'd want to do things for themselves when they can too."

I couldn't argue with that. I just wished my best friend could go. "He'd love this so much," I said.

"Tell you what we *will* do," Dad said. "Let's tell Thomas that if he saves enough money for camp next year, we'll let him use Jason's bike that week."

"He'd love that. He was thinking he'd have to save enough for camp and for renting a bike too."

"I think saving for camp alone will give him enough of a sense of accomplishment," Dad said. "Maybe knowing a bike comes with that will help motivate him."

I couldn't wait to tell Thomas, and when I did, he was thrilled.

The Sunday we were to leave for camp, Thomas got permission to go to church with us, have dinner with us, and ride along to Muskegon. Dad would then take him back to Lake Farm.

We were going to have a carful. We didn't even have room for Mom and Kate, because Dad had offered to take Daniel and Jonathan too. That was four boys and three bikes. We were pretty crammed in there.

Actually I was glad to be able to say my good-byes to Kate and Mom at home. Mom knows I hate to be hugged and kissed in public, but she thinks it's funny to do it anyway. "No way you're going to get too big or too old to love your mama," she would tease, and then I would have to let her hug me and give me a peck on the cheek.

I didn't have to worry about that with Kate. We hardly even said good-bye to each other, and we never admitted we missed each other. Maybe she didn't miss me, but I did miss her. That always surprised me, but it was true, even more so since Jason had been gone.

The funniest sight of the day was Jonathan showing up at our house on his bike, somehow carrying a sleeping bag and a big old suitcase. His hair flopped in the breeze, and he was weaving all over the road. We saw him from the dining room during dessert, and it gave us a good laugh. He stashed his stuff next to the station wagon and came in the back door.

"I don't suppose you'd be interested in polishing off this leftover piece of strawberry shortcake," Mom said.

"Oh, I really couldn't," Jonathan said in a high voice, pretending to be his mom on a diet. "I just had a big lunch." But while he was saying that, he was also accepting the dessert and starting to eat it.

"Well, at least sit down," Mom said.

"Uh-uh," Jonathan managed with his mouth full. "We're running late, aren't we, Mr. Andrews?"

Dad shook his head and pointed to a chair. "You've got a few minutes while I get the bikes on top of the car."

On our way out of town we stopped to pick up Daniel Jackson. I always loved being at his house because his father was a huge black man with a deep voice and a great sense of humor. He was sales manager for a car dealership and had offered to let my dad use a van to get us all to camp. Dad said he would have accepted but that the bike rack was already on our car, and though we would be crowded, we'd be fine. Mr. Jackson insisted on picking us up the next Saturday.

"I'll be bringing a big ol' van," he said, "in case you boys eat like you did at church camp last year! Toby, if you see Daniel riding off in the wrong direction, just remember where you saw him last, and we'll track him down in a month or so, OK?"

I never knew how to answer Mr. Jackson. He was always

kidding, but he also always wanted an answer, so I just laughed and nodded.

"I'm counting on you now, son," he said.

The Jacksons were sure not shy about showing *their* affection in public. Daniel hugged and kissed his father, his mother, his two older brothers, and his older sister. He looked a little embarrassed, but I guess he was used to it and knew there was no getting out of it anyway. They really seemed like a loving family, everybody telling Daniel to have a good time.

When we got to the camp in Muskegon, we were disappointed to find that the three of us were all in different cabins and on different teams. We would be together for big meetings and things, but most of the biking activities were done with your own team.

We were told that the camp was so successful last year that they were planning on having a whole summer of bike camps for different ages. The only risk in the spring was the weather, of course, but we were lucky most of the week. The only day we couldn't ride was Tuesday, when it poured all day and we stayed inside and watched movies during free time.

Each team had its own cabin and counselor. I felt the luckiest of the three Junior Deputies, because my counselor, Jimmy Fritz, was actually a stunt cyclist, sponsored by a big bicycle manufacturer. He said there were other Christians on the stunt riding circuit but that he was the only one who also spoke and did camps like this one.

Besides being our counselor, he also spoke two nights to the whole group, once about his own life and how he became a Christian and once about how to live as a Christian when you're surrounded by people who don't believe what you believe.

For someone who had won lots of motocross races when he was younger and was famous on the stunt circuit now, Jimmy sure seemed like a humble guy. He was good-looking and successful, and he was going to college too. He could have been conceited and cocky, but he really seemed genuine. For the kids who had the right kinds of bikes—I didn't—Jimmy did a special workshop on stunt riding. The rest of us just watched while the other kids started slow and gradually learned to do some of Jimmy's simpler tricks. It was amazing. After he got everybody convinced that safety was most important and showed them how easy some tricks were that looked hard, he gave a demonstration.

He popped a cassette into a tape player and went through a routine to the music. You had to see it to believe it. He could walk all over the place on his bike without even making the tires go around. He would jerk back and stand on the rear wheel, the front tire high off the ground as if he were riding a bucking bronco.

Then he would lurch forward and balance on the front tire while the back was in the air. Then he would walk the bike that way, front to back, back to front, all over the place. Next he stood perfectly still on both wheels, with them straight in line, balancing. He didn't move an inch. Nobody could figure out how he did that, and though everybody tried, nobody could match it.

He admitted that there were only a few professional stunt riders who could do that. "It's just a knack I have, I guess," he said.

Jimmy set up several orange plastic cones in a line, too close together to maneuver between unless you were Jimmy Fritz. He backed up and got a good speed going, then started to weave through the cones. Just when it looked as if there was no way he could make the next tight turn, he stopped dead and hopped, turning the bike in the air and landing in the direction he needed to go.

We all clapped and cheered, and that seemed to get him going all the more.

By the end of the week, we all wanted to be like Jimmy.

He encouraged us to do our best, not just on our bikes but also in school, in church and Sunday school, at home, in our own private Bible reading and prayer, and everything. My favorite part of the camp week, not counting what happened on the weekend, was the cabin devotions every night before lights out. I don't know where Jimmy got all of his knowledge. I mean, he wasn't a pastor or anything, but he sure knew the Bible.

He would take a few verses or a chapter and have us read it and talk about it, and then he would apply it to our lives. I have to admit, I believed the Bible, but I had never realized how practical somebody could make it. He would read verses and then compare them to some everyday situation, and we would all see that if we were really going to call ourselves Christians, we would have to live the way the Bible said.

Best of all, as far as biking was concerned, Jimmy also had great ideas on how we could win the camp competitions in speed races, bike hiking, and even scavenger hunting. We were so far ahead by Friday that we could have finished last in the combination map and compass scavenger hunt and still have won the overall team prize.

It was a good thing too, because I got sidetracked and basically dropped out of the competition, leaving it to my teammates to try to win while worrying about where I was. But my little side trip was worth it. It would become the second big case for the Kalamazoo County Junior Deputies.

The Game

Icouldn't believe the week had gone so quickly. Everything pointed to the big day, Friday, when the teams would race all over the city of Muskegon and surrounding communities.

Every guy on each team had a special assignment. Your sheet told you where to go and what to bring back, but it was all in code. We had all been taught how to read the clues, and those who hadn't caught on were assigned to ride along with others.

In our cabin, everybody learned because Jimmy would not settle for anything less. A couple of the guys were still struggling Thursday night, but he spent time with each of them until they were ready to go on their own.

First, the whole camp assembled in the dining hall. Rather than sitting down for a meal as we usually did, we lined up and made our own sack lunches from stuff provided at the tables. You could make sandwiches and take snack bars and stuff like that, but you had to make sure you could carry it and not smash it before lunchtime. Each assignment would take no less than five hours, so everybody carried food and water and a spare tire. We were also instructed to wear hats and use sunscreen and bug spray.

The fun thing about the assignments was that none of them would take anybody more than fifteen or twenty miles from camp, but we would all ride dozens of miles before we finished our task. My assignment was to follow a route and stop for further instructions at eight different checkpoints. At each point I would get directions to the next spot. Finally, at the last place, I would pick up whatever was waiting for me and deliver it back to the camp.

The guys in charge told us that if you knew exactly where to go and in what order, and you were healthy and strong and had a good bike and rode top speed all the way, you might possibly complete your personal course in a little over five hours. The record was five hours and twenty-four minutes.

The funny thing was, if it worked right, most of us would be stopping at the same sites at one time or another. But just because you saw a camper on his bike stopping for instructions, you couldn't just go straight there and do the same. You had to get your own instructions in order, and you had to present each clue at the end too.

They warned us that some of the clues would be more difficult than others. Some guys would get stuck on one and never get any further, but most of us would eventually finish the course. If we weren't finished within a half hour before dark, we were to head back.

It wasn't as much fun for the other teams, because our team had clinched the week's overall prize on the obstacle course the night before.

Poor Jonathan. He was leading and had the best time before he missed a short ramp, flipped, and skinned his elbow. Knowing him, I was sure he was more upset about losing than about getting hurt.

Daniel got hurt during the week too, but it was during free time. Some of the guys found a hill on the campgrounds that led from some private mobile homes all the way down to the parking lot. There was a speed bump near the bottom, to discourage people from driving too fast into the lot. But there was a groove cut out of the middle of the bump so bikes could go through without flipping. It was still dangerous, though, because even if you missed the bump, you still flashed past some trees that blocked your view of cars and their view of you.

When I saw Daniel with his hands and arms all bandaged up, I got the story.

"All the other sissies coasted down that hill," he said. "They got up some pretty good speed, but what's the fun of that? I started pedaling right from the top. Man, I was cruising by the time I got near that speed bump. I was goin' so fast I didn't know if I could steer through the little opening or not. If I had hit the bump, I would have gone flying. About a second before the bump, I quit pedaling, because I was going too fast as it was.

"There were guys at the bottom watching for cars, but even if they had told me a car was coming, there was no stopping then. They would have done better to try to flag down the car, which was what they tried to do.

"I saw them waving at me and waving to where a car must have been coming, and I didn't know what to do. I knew if I tried to slam on the brakes, I would slide. Then I wondered if I should start pedaling again to try to beat the car.

"Finally I just decided to aim right through the opening and take my chances. It felt like I was goin' forty down that hill, but all of a sudden everything was like in slow motion. I could hear the guys talking about how fast I was going and that I was going to kill myself.

"I wanted to shut my eyes. I didn't want to see a car if one

43

was really going to hit me. As I flew through the opening and past the trees, I could see out of the corner of my eye that the car had stopped, and I went whizzing past. Only now I was going so fast I couldn't make the curve in the parking lot. I was heading for the big rock that keeps cars from driving on the grass.

"I knew I had to miss that, so I leaned left and tried to turn. I could feel the back tire start to slide, but when I tried to straighten up, the bike jerked to the right and threw me right over that rock. I bounced in the grass and then onto the asphalt. That's how I got so torn up. Wait till you see my palms and my knuckles."

"But you're all right?"

He nodded. "Yeah. It was almost worth it, but I was scared. They said I was talking as I flew through the air."

"What were you saying?"

"I have no idea, but they said it sounded like a prayer. I wish I had the guts to try that run again."

"How's your bike?"

"It'll be fine by tomorrow's race."

And it was.

I saw Jonathan's and Daniel's teams take off, all riding together to the first corner and then heading in different directions.

Jimmy gave our team last-minute instructions, reminding us that lots of the clues would be plays on words. Others would be more obvious.

"Give each one a lot of thought," he said. "We don't need this race, but we want it. Let's win. They count the order of our finishes and add them up. Lowest score wins. Let's do it!"

We were each handed our first assignment sheet. Mine simply said, "Dry dock prescriptions."

What in the world did that mean? I stood there staring at it, hoping something would come to me or that other words would miraculously appear on the page.

"Remember," Jimmy hollered, "you've done enough riding around town that you should eventually recognize every clue."

I had to give this some thought.

"Think about it while you're riding," he said. "Nothing is at the camp—you know that."

I rode slowly, holding onto the handlebar with one hand and reading the note in my other hand. Dry dock. A boat that's not in the water. Prescriptions. That's what you get at a drugstore. I stuffed the paper into my pocket and smacked myself in the head. I hoped they were all this easy.

I had seen a boat in someone's yard in town. It faced a little shopping strip across the street. I didn't know if there was a drugstore in that strip, but if there was I was on my way. I wanted to win this race. I could figure stuff out, and I could ride as well as anyone else in the camp. I had finished second in the distance race and third in the sprint, and no one else had finished that high in both.

I raced past the boat in the yard and slid to a stop, scanning the strip mall. Sure enough, there was a drugstore. Now where would I find my clue? There was nothing in the parking lot or outside the door. I locked my bike on a rack and hurried in. I could tell from the amused looks on the faces of the clerks that they were expecting me.

"Anyone want to tell me where my clue is?" I said.

"Can't," they said. "You're on your own."

"Oh, brother," I said. "Not even a clue? Am I warm? Do I stay in here or go back out?"

No one would say anything, so I looked all around. I looked up in the corners, behind the mirrors, down each row. Finally, right in the middle of a huge stack of blue coffee cans, under a sign that said "Dry goods," I saw a red coffee can. It was clearly in the wrong place, and it was right at eye level. I shook it and heard no coffee grounds. The plastic lid came off easily and revealed dozens of cards, each addressed differently.

I finally found one that read, "Jimmy's team, rider MB." That was me. I turned the card over. It said simply, "s'egraM." Now there was a puzzle.

I replaced the lid and the can and hurried out to my bike, clutching my second clue. While I ran the strange word over and over in my mind, I unlocked my bike to save time.

As I was climbing aboard, I looked again at the card. The word didn't mean anything to me, but why would there be an apostrophe near the beginning and a capital letter at the end? The word was backward! I read it from right to left. "Marge's." That was the name of the laundromat across the parking lot.

But at first I could find nothing near or in the place that led me to another clue. As I scanned the washers and dryers and vending machines, I had no idea where I might find a can with clues in it. I sat in a yellow plastic chair to think and continue looking.

All the machines were the same, but the last big dryer against the wall had a little "Out of Order" sign on it. Was that a clue? I thought about it. Something worked at the edges of my mind.

As I walked toward the dryer, I knew I would find something inside. Maybe the dryer was really out of order, and maybe it wasn't. But the *clue* had been out of the (right) order: the letters were backward! I opened the dryer, and there it was! I peeled off the top of the can and found my next card.

It read, "People are dying to get in here, but you may fall short."

We were not allowed to mislead the other teams, but we had permission to tip off our own teammates if we saw any of them struggling. I went outside and looked up and down the street, hoping to see someone on my team. I saw several guys from other teams, including a couple of kids sliding up to the drugstore.

One kid walked slowly to Marge's and said, "Where'd you get that card?"

"Like I'm going to tell you," I said, smiling. "You'll figure it out."

I needed to be riding, heading somewhere, but I didn't want to shoot off in the wrong direction and have to backtrack. I ran through my mind some of the things I knew were down each street. A lot of kids were riding north, but the only thing that way was a movie theater and then some farmland before you arrived at the cemetery.

I straddled my bike and stood there, staring at my card. People die before they get into a cemetery, I realized. And off I raced.

When I got there I found three or four guys from different teams walking in and around the gravestones. "How'd you get in there?" I hollered. The gate was closed, and the fence high.

"We climbed that big tree and dropped down over the fence!"

I looked at the tree, and something didn't seem right. It didn't make sense that they would want a bunch of kids roaming through a cemetery. I looked at my clue again. "You may fall short." Did that mean I might or that I had permission to?

A shorter tree stood right next to the one the boys had climbed. I moseyed over to it, acting as if I were sizing up the big tree for climbing. I sneaked a peek at the others. They were busy running up and down the rows of tombstones. I searched the short tree and found the can of clues between the branches. I quickly pocketed mine and raced off, which tipped off the others that they were looking in the wrong place.

"Hey!" they hollered. "Did you find it? Where is it?"

One said, "He's bluffing. Scared to climb the tree."

I had no idea when they might find what I found.

My next clue was simple to figure out but not easy to chase down. It led me more than six miles the other way. It read, "Don't flog yourself if you can't figure out this rough one. Of course, it could be a trap, Ace."

"Rough, course, trap, and *ace* are all golfing terms, and *flog* is *golf* backwards." The only golf course within the boundaries of our hunt was a private course all the way on the other side of town. I had a feeling I was making good time, figuring clues quickly, and had a chance of winning if I kept up the pace. It had been only a half hour or so, and I was almost halfway through my clues.

So I set off for the golf course, not knowing I had found my last clue of the day. At least in that game.

Seeing Things

It took quite a while to get to the private golf course on the other side of Muskegon. A lot of the way was uphill, and, because of some road construction, I had to detour through a long stretch that was dirt and gravel. That's the hardest surface to ride on, except sand, of course, which is impossible.

By the time I finally got to the course, the day was dry and hot, and the sun was high in the sky. I pulled under a tree and put some sunscreen on and pulled my hat out of my bag. I wasn't hungry yet, but I drank about half my water. I had been riding long enough. I walked my bike up to the entrance, and then I had a sinking feeling.

It was one thing for a store or a laundromat to let the camp hide clues in their places, but would a private golf club? Was there a public course somewhere close by that I didn't know about? Or how about a miniature golf course or a driving range? I sure hoped I was wrong, because I had come a long way out of my way for this.

As I waited by the entrance I didn't see any other campers, and there sure didn't seem to be any coffee cans sitting around. That would have looked tacky at such a fancy place. Most of the golfers ignored me, but some looked disgustedly at me, as though I wasn't supposed to be there.

One man said, "If you're looking for the caddie sign-up, it's next to the pro shop."

I wasn't looking to sign up to be a caddie, but I just thanked him and said nothing else. I didn't want to say I was looking for clues. I hung around, trying to stay out of the way while trying to see where the clues might be. There didn't seem to be any way I could get into the place unless I was pretending to be a caddie, and I didn't want to lie.

After a while I walked my bike back out of the entrance and along the fence that protected the golf course from the road. That fence also protected cars from golf balls, I guess, but I think the private club was more worried about non-members getting in than golf balls getting out.

I was sweating through my clothes as I made my way down the road, looking forward to a little shade every few hundred feet when there was a tree. It was fun to watch the players, some good and some not. I had never played, but I could tell the difference between someone who knew what he was doing and one who didn't. I knew that much just from listening to my brother talk about it. He had been a caddie and a golf fan.

Some guys were hitting the ball all over the place and having to find it in tall grass or among trees. And then there were some who always seemed to hit it straight and put it right where they wanted.

One of the holes had its green near the fence, so I parked under a tree and sat in the shade, resting and watching as groups of four came through and tried to putt their golf balls into the hole. They sure seemed to be having fun.

It was kind of fun to sit there watching, realizing that no

one could see me. Because of the way the sun cast a shadow of the branches, I was in a spot where people could seem to look right at me and not see me or my bike. I just sat there listening to their conversations and trying to guess how many shots it would take them to sink the ball.

I decided to watch one more group play the hole before marching back to the entrance and just asking someone whether I was at the right or wrong place. I had wasted enough time on this trip. If I was at the wrong place, I wanted to know now so I could get back on track and maybe still win the thing. I was finally getting hungry too.

I was at a place where I could see the golfers tee off from maybe four or five hundred yards away. Then, after they hit their second or third shots, I lost sight of them because of a dip in the land until they came up to hit their shots onto this green. Then they might shoot three or four putts each or sometimes just one or two if they were good. It seemed that the better they played, the less they swore.

I saw four men tee off and then go after their balls, two of them looking for theirs in the woods, the other two on the fairway. When the four of them came up over the rise, I squinted, wondering if I was seeing things.

Who was that third guy to try to shoot onto the green? He wore navy shorts and a red shirt. He had dark hair and looked as if he would be bald in a few years. He wore glasses. He looked like someone I knew. Who was it?

I stared at him, ignoring the others. What a coincidence! Somebody I knew! I was just sure of it. But who was it? A relative? A friend? Someone from church? Someone my dad worked with? A teacher from school? Where did I know this guy from?

His golf ball was just a few feet off the green on the far side from me. He tried to loft it up toward the hole, but he hit it too hard, and the ground was too dry to slow it down. It skipped past the hole and rolled toward the fence, going

51

between two bushes and stopping out of sight of the golfer and within ten feet of me. Of course, I was outside the fence in the shadow, so now I would be able to get a good look at the man without his seeing me.

He was muttering as he switched clubs and walked around the green to find his ball. I wanted to tell him where it was, but I knew there were some kind of manners in golf that said you weren't supposed to talk while someone was playing. I didn't know enough to know whether that meant only while someone was swinging or not, so I thought it was best to just keep quiet.

When the man came into view, I knew even from his profile that I was right. I knew him for sure, and if I could just come up with where I knew him from, I could remember his name. He looked at the lie of his golf ball and swore. Then he seemed to look right into my face as he came around to the roadside of his shot.

And I remembered. I knew. I hadn't been able to put it together because it was the last place I would have expected to see him. But he was Max Carney from the Lake Farm Home. He must have been on vacation.

We weren't friends, of course. In fact, he might not even remember me. And even if he did, I couldn't imagine he would be thrilled to see me. But who knew? Maybe when he was away from his job and having fun he was a friendlier guy. He seemed to get along with the other players.

Now I *really* wanted to say something, but I decided to wait until after his shot. He was crouched and leaning over and saying something about reading the green. He wasn't using a putter but some kind of a wedge or an iron with an angled head on it.

Mr. Carney waited, hunched over, until the others cleared out of his vision. Then he lifted a gentle shot that bounced once on the green and rolled straight toward the hole. I stood and watched as it rolled around the cup and out. Mr. Carney danced and shouted, and everyone laughed at his reaction to how close he had come.

I was about to greet him, but he ran onto the green, sort of showing off. Then he leaned over and tapped the ball in, said something about shooting par, and headed back to his golf cart. I was too embarrassed to call out to him then, and, besides, I knew I had to get going. He was heading off to the next tee, which was not near the road.

I wondered if there were any more tees or greens near the road. It would be silly to run into someone you sort of knew so far from home and not say hi.

I headed back toward the clubhouse, where I wandered in unnoticed. I'm sure anyone who did see me just assumed I was a caddie or looking for an application to be one.

I asked a man in the pro shop if he knew anything about the bicycle race from the camp. He didn't, but he pointed me to someone who would know if anything like that was going on.

The man behind the counter at the front desk told me he was aware of the race. "We were asked to participate but had to say no because of our tournament here today."

"So this isn't just some part of the clue that I'm supposed to try to figure out."

He smiled. "No, I'm afraid not. Sorry."

"Is there another golf course in Muskegon?"

"Several."

"How about a public course?"

He told me how to get to one about four miles away. I knew my chances of winning the race were probably gone by now. "My brother was a caddie. He used to work the club tournaments."

"That's exactly what we have going today," the man said. "We don't need any caddies, but you can leave an application for the future."

"Thanks, I don't live around here," I said. "What *is* a club tournament anyway?"

"That's where everyone in the tournament has to be a member. No guests today—no out-of-towners."

"Really? You have members from as far away as I live?"

"Which is—"

"Kalamazoo."

"Oh, no. I think our member from the farthest away is a woman from Lansing."

"I just saw a guy from Kalamazoo playing."

"I don't think so," the man said. "No nonmembers today, like I said."

"This guy's name is Carney. Max Carney. He works at—"

"You must have been mistaken, son," the man said kindly. "I know every member, and we've never had a Carney."

"But I saw him!"

The man was still smiling, but I was sure I was becoming a pest. "Like I said, you must have mistaken him for someone else."

"Is there anyplace besides just down the way here where a tee or a green is near the road and I can get a better look at him?"

The man's smile faded, and he sighed. "There's a schematic—you know what that is?"

"No, sir."

"An aerial view of the course that shows how we're laid out. When did you see him at the ninth hole?"

"I don't know if it was the ninth."

"If it was out here in front near the fence, it was the ninth."

"Just before I came in here."

"Then you should be able to see him on the tee at the thirteenth in forty-five to sixty minutes. And the green on the fifteenth hole is by the fence too, if you want to look at it. But stay outside and don't talk to the players, please."

I looked at the schematic, as he called it, and it showed a long bike ride around the outside of the course to those two spots. Now I had to decide whether to forget about the camp race and find out if it was Mr. Carney.

The longer I sat thinking about it on a bench out in front, the hungrier I got. I ate my lunch, realizing that all the time I was spending thinking about this was really making my decision for me. I didn't have any idea whether the public course was the right place to go either. I could be on a wild-goose chase.

Anyway, curiosity got the best of me. I would go and camp out at the thirteenth hole, out of sight again if I could, and I would only say hi to Mr. Carney, nothing else. That seemed innocent enough.

I rode my bike out onto the road, taking my time getting to the next corner and turning toward the thirteenth hole. On the way, I had some fun. In my mirror I caught sight of a group of about six cyclists way behind me, heading toward the club entrance. I knew they could see me, so I speeded up as if I were still in the race and had something up my sleeve.

I didn't know whether they'd think I had already found my clue and was heading off to my next destination or if I seemed to know where the clues were. I saw them stop near the entrance and watch me, then they turned in. But the last rider looked like a kid from our team! I couldn't let him make the same mistake I had.

I waved at him, but he didn't see me. I waited until they had all had time to get near the entrance, then I raced back and skidded to a stop, watching them begin locking up their bikes.

"Buddy," I called softly, and the young boy looked up. I put a finger to my lips so he wouldn't tip off the others, and he came running over.

"Bring your bike," I whispered.

When he got his bike, the others noticed. They knew I knew something, and they also knew I would be telling him. They wanted to go wherever I told him to go. He was next to me with his bike ready to roll. They were unlocking theirs.

"This is the wrong place," I whispered. "I think it's the public course, three miles east and one mile north. Hurry."

He flew out of there, with the others shouting and laughing, trying to unlock their bikes and catch up. They were all going somewhere I was no longer interested in. I wanted to see Max Carney again.

My "Mistake"

I didn't have as good a spot to spy on Max Carney near the thirteenth tee as I had had on the ninth green. To stay out of sight I had to be about twenty feet to the left of the tee, behind the fence and a large bush. There was no reason to hide, really, but I didn't want to make a fool of myself, and the man in the clubhouse, the one who knew all the members, had asked me not to talk to the players.

I wasn't going to bother Mr. Carney. I was just going to say hi to him. Most of all, I wanted to take back to Thomas Christian the surprising news that the seemingly dull and lifeless Max Carney actually played golf in his spare time. I doubted that Thomas had ever seen the man smile, let alone play or have any fun.

It was almost an hour from when I had seen Mr. Carney on the ninth green that he and his partners pulled up in two golf carts to wait for their turns at the tee.

I had to admit that Carney didn't sound like himself. I had never heard him raise his voice at Lake Farm. Of course, I hadn't seen that much of him. But all the times he talked to Thomas or my dad or me, he spoke in that quiet, disgusted tone, as if the last thing he wanted to do was waste time explaining rules to us.

Yet here he was, laughing and joking with friends. The backs of my legs were burning as I crouched behind a bush, trying to hear what they were saying.

One said something about how slow the play went when so many players were in a tournament.

"I know," Max Carney said. "We usually get around the course in about half this time. And they tried to schedule it pretty well. Just didn't work."

"It usually takes us this long," another said, "with Fred chasing his shots into the water and the woods and over the road!"

They all laughed.

Then Max Carney said, "Well, I'm not always that bad. Last week I missed a hole-in-one by six strokes."

They laughed so hard I thought one of them was going to fall out of the cart. He reached over and slapped Max Carney on the shoulder and said, "Fred, you are something else!"

Fred?

So he *wasn't* Max Carney! What an idiot I had been! I couldn't believe I had been chasing around the edge of a private golf club, miles away from where I was supposed to be, watching a club member named Fred because I thought he looked like Max Carney! How could I be so stupid?

I thought about racing over to the public course, but by now I would be so late it would be useless. Maybe I should just head back to camp and tell Jimmy Fritz I had messed up and that there was no sense in finishing. Except that I knew how he'd react. He wouldn't be mad at me or tell me off. But he would insist on my finishing the course.

To Jimmy, quitting was never an option. I could just hear him saying, "I wouldn't be doing my job as your counselor if

I let you quit. You owe it to the rest of the guys to finish so we're not disqualified."

Just thinking about that made me realize that I was going to have to apologize to everyone if I didn't get back on course. That would be no fun. Even worse, I would have to admit that I had been wrong in the first place. Thinking I had seen someone I knew had cost me a couple of hours, and I had been wrong anyway.

I stretched and stood, reaching for my bike.

But this Fred guy, the one who looked so much like Max Carney, was getting ready to tee off. As he pushed his tee into the ground, he picked up a broken-off head of a tee and turned to flip it away, which caused him to face my direction.

Because I was now standing, he saw me and did a little double take, looking me full in the face. If that wasn't Max Carney, I was the Easter bunny! I almost said something, and I thought I saw in his eyes that he seemed to recognize me. But then he turned back to his shot as if he had seen right through me.

Was it just my imagination, or was he working hard at ignoring me, the kid on the other side of the fence? Wouldn't it have been natural for him to glance at me again while his friends were shooting?

But he didn't. He positioned himself with his back to me the whole time, then put his club away and climbed into the cart again. In a few minutes, they were heading down the fairway.

Now I didn't know what to do. There was no chance of winning the race or even helping my team win it, though I thought I should finish. Yet I wanted another look at this Fred guy. Why was this bothering me so much? Why did I care? I didn't know. I had never seen anybody who looked so much like somebody else. At least this guy had to be Max Carney's twin! Still, the guy at the clubhouse had said there were no

Carneys in the membership. Who ever heard of twins with different last names!

I stood beside my bike for several minutes, thinking about giving this up and finishing the race, even if I was dead last. That would be the easiest. But what kind of Junior Deputy would I be? Dad had always told me that a lot of police work is following your hunches, getting all your questions and suspicions answered, and following leads.

This was too confusing, but I knew it would bug me forever if I didn't find the truth.

The next foursome came to the tee, and a woman knelt to pick up a yarn mitt, the cover that goes over the club head. "Hey, somebody left this here," she said, turning it over and studying it. "It says 'Fred Anthony' on it. Anybody know a Fred Anthony?"

"I do," one of the men said. "He's just ahead of us. Who's teeing off fourth?"

His friend said he was.

"Why don't you run this down to Fred before you shoot? They're just down there."

The other man hesitated, as if he didn't want to be bothered.

I suddenly had a flash. "Give it to me," I said. "I'll give it to him when he gets to the green at fifteen."

The foursome turned as one and stared at me.

"You're going to fifteen?" the woman said.

"Yeah. Here, I'll give it to him."

She looked at the others, who shrugged, seeming happy to be able to forget about it. She tossed the mitt over the fence to me, and I rode off to the fifteenth green.

The golf head mitt was brightly colored with a yellow body and red tassel on top. The name "Fred Anthony" had been sewn onto it, also in red. I knew all I would have to do would be to stand in plain sight by the fence and wave that mitt, and this Fred Anthony would recognize it. I had a few minutes to think of what to say.

But when Fred Anthony's foursome approached the green, he ignored me again. One of his partners saw me waving the club mitt and said, "Hey, Fred, isn't that yours?"

Fred glanced my way and said, "Yeah. Get it for me, will ya?"

The man came over and reached for the mitt.

"I kinda wanted to give it to Max myself."

"To *who?*"

"Max. That *is* Max Carney, isn't it?"

"No, that's Fred Anthony. See? That's what it says on the mitt."

"Well, still, I'd like to give it to him myself."

"Just give it to me, kid. What do you think—he's gonna give you a tip or something?"

"No."

"Where'd you get this, anyway?"

"At the thirteenth tee."

"Were you inside the fence?"

"No, another player found it, and I offered to run it over here."

"Well, thanks. Just give it here."

I shouldn't have, but I just tossed it over the fence. I watched as the man took it to Fred Anthony and told him what I had said. Fred flinched like he was surprised, but he didn't look over at me. He just laughed as if whatever he had just heard was silly and took the mitt to his cart. On the way he waved and said, "Thanks, kid!" but still he didn't look at me.

"You're welcome, Max!" I hollered, and finally I got him to look quickly at me and then look away—though that's something he would have done whether he was really Max Carney or really Fred Anthony. I wasn't getting anywhere, but I *was* being bold.

The other three players turned to him. "What'd he call you?" one asked.

Max/Fred pointed to his head and wiggled his finger, like I was some sort of nut.

They laughed and played on.

Now I was hooked. I wanted to talk to this guy and see him close up. I knew I would be able to tell for sure then. If this guy wasn't really Max Carney, he looked enough like him that he ought to at least know about it. I would be happy to tell him. If I looked that much like somebody else, I'd want to know. I would even want to meet the person. Now, where would I be able to see him again?

When Fred Anthony's foursome completed the fifteenth hole, they would have only three to go. I remembered from the schematic aerial view of the course that no more of the tees or greens were near the road. One fairway was within sight, but unless Fred Anthony shot a ball way into the rough by the fence, I would not get close to him. If I didn't see him again, how would I ever track him down to talk to him face-to-face? I could look him up in the phone book, but he wouldn't have to talk to me.

I raced back to the clubhouse, the sun beating down on me. I locked my bike in a rack at the front, where I noticed that the other three or four bikes there were very expensive and that the owners had taken the front tires into the clubhouse with them to help protect against theft. I wondered how these rich people carried their golf bags when they rode their bikes to the club.

I slipped inside and went right to the schematic. I ran my finger along the drawing to show where Fred Anthony and his friends would be right about now. They had to finish sixteen, seventeen, and eighteen, and then where would they go? That would put them near the practice putting greens, which lay alongside a path that led to The Nineteenth Hole Lounge.

I walked through the back of the clubhouse to see the

place. The lounge was mostly a bar, but there were also places to sit and eat, and it even had a large seating area outside where waiters and waitresses delivered food and drinks. A sign at the entrance, which faced the path near those practice putting greens, said, "Members and invited guests only. No one under 18 admitted."

No way I was going to just walk in there.

I looked around and noticed that the caddies seemed to be only a little older than I was and dressed about the same. My problem was that I looked a little worn out and sloppy to be a caddie. So I ducked into a washroom and splashed cold water on my face and hair, toweled off, brushed my hair into place, tucked my shirt in, and pulled up my pants.

Now I thought I could pass as a caddie, but of course that still wouldn't get me into the lounge, through which Fred Anthony would at least have to pass, even if he didn't stop. It appeared to me that he would have to go through the outside part of the lounge to get to the locker room. That's where everyone else seemed to go after they finished their rounds.

I went back to the schematic and noticed there seemed to be a path behind the practice greens, leading around the lounge and toward the open air area. If I could get back in there unnoticed, I would be shielded by the pro shop on one side and shrubbery on the other. I would have a clear view of anyone who came through the outside part of the lounge. Now, was that what it really looked like, or was that only an old rendering by an artist?

Well, the rendering must have been done years before, when the shrubbery was short and new. Now it was years later, and the bushes had grown higher. The place would be better for hiding than it looked on the drawing! I didn't want to wait in a cramped spot between shrubs and pro shop for longer than I needed to. That would be uncomfortable, especially in the heat. But I didn't want to risk missing the Max Carney look-alike either.

I busied myself walking around and window shopping at the pro shop, trying my best to look like a caddie.

Unfortunately, I was a little too good at it, especially for someone who knew so little about golf. A man came up to me and asked if I was looking for caddying work the following Saturday.

"Sorry," I said, "I don't live around here."

"I could make it worth your while," he said. "I'm a big tipper."

It was almost tempting. I could have used the money. But I had to tell him no. He'd have been pretty disappointed in my caddying.

Talking to him almost made me miss what I was there for. Over his shoulder I could see the foursome coming, the one that included a man named Fred Anthony, who looked enough like Max Carney to be his twin.

Face to Face

I nearly ran into a golf cart trying to keep an eye on Fred Anthony as he and his party made their way through the back of the clubhouse and into the lounge. Then I jogged between pro shop and shrubs and waited to see if they would walk through the outside seating area. No one could see me.

For a few minutes I was afraid I had been mistaken and that they had found another way to the locker room. Then I noticed them inside, sitting together at the bar. I waited, knowing they would still have to come my way. Would they stop and sit at a table, or would I get one more chance to look at this guy's face as he passed?

I got tired of waiting, but eventually they came out. One went on into the locker room, but Fred and the other two sat at a table, where a waiter soon came and took their order. He came back with sandwiches a few minutes later, and the men sat teasing each other about their game and pretending to argue over whose turn it was to pay.

It must have been Fred's because when the other two

finished eating, they left too, leaving him sitting there alone. He seemed to be just relaxing. I wasn't that far from him, and I became convinced more than ever that he had to be Max Carney. Finally, I talked myself into saying something.

"Mr. Carney?" I called out.

He jerked his head up and stared at me.

"Excuse me, but aren't you Max Carney from Kalamazoo?"

"You again?" he said. And though he was louder than I had ever heard Max Carney, I thought he sounded like him too. "No, I'm not from Kalamazoo."

He turned away again, but I had come too far to be brushed off now. I pushed my way through the bushes and stepped over a one-foot fence that looked like it was designed to keep out puppies.

"Sir?" I said, as he looked up in disgust. "Are you really not Max Carney from Kalamazoo? You don't work at the Lake Farm Home?"

He looked directly at me, and I had the feeling I was looking into the eyes of Max Carney.

"No, I am not whoever you said, and I am not from Kalamazoo. I've been there, but I've never lived there. And I've never heard of this farm or whatever it is."

"Lake Farm," I said, and then I did something I can't even explain. I asked if he minded if I sat down a second.

"Yes, I do mind," he said. "I have appointments this afternoon and have to get going soon."

I sat down anyway. "I don't want to bother you, sir," I said, thrusting out my hand.

He reluctantly shook it and said, "Fred. Fred Anthony."

"But there's a man in Kalamazoo, like I said, a man named Max Carney, who looks so much like you that you could be twins. Has anyone ever told you that before?"

He shook his head, still irritated and looking like he had to get going. "Never," he said. "Now if you'll excuse me—"

"Well, sure, but really, if you're ever in Kalamazoo you should look this guy up. I mean you wouldn't believe it. You'd think you were looking in a mirror. He works at the Lake Farm Home on Oakland Drive."

He stood and began moving away.

"Really, you ought to look him up."

"Yeah, well, maybe," he said as he headed for the locker room.

Now I was totally baffled. The closer I was to him, the more I was convinced that he and Max Carney were one and the same person. But why would he lie? He probably would have recognized me if he was Carney. I didn't mention Thomas Christian's name, because the man claimed he had never even heard of Lake Farm. What was this?

"Did you want something, son?" the waiter said, and I realized where I was.

"Oh, no, I was just talking to the man who was here."

"Mr. Anthony?"

"Uh, yeah. You know him?"

"Sure do," the waiter said. "He's been a member for years. Good guy, good tipper." He picked up the check Carney/Anthony had left on the table. "Never knew him to walk out on a bill though. No problem. We'll just put it on his tab. We do it all the time."

"You know there's a man where I live, in Kalamazoo, that looks exactly like him."

"Like Fred? No kiddin'? He's not the most common-looking guy, is he? Interesting. By the way, you're really not supposed to be in here if you're not with somebody."

And he walked away.

As I rode away from the golf course, I realized I didn't even know if the public course was where I was supposed to go for my next clue. I rode to where I had been told it was, and all that was there was a driving range.

I asked if this was where the bike race clues were

supposed to be. "You don't have to tell me where they are," I told the teenager behind the counter. "Just tell me if I'm at the right place or not."

"You're about the twentieth guy I've told today," he said. "You're in the wrong place. I'm not supposed to tell you, but it's on the other side of Muskegon."

I thanked him, but there was no way I was going that far. That would be twice as far as I'd come already, and this was already a lost cause. I headed back to camp, knowing I would get a lecture from Jimmy Fritz.

He wasn't around when I got there about an hour later. It was getting late in the afternoon, and a couple of kids had returned, either hurt or with two flat tires, sick, or simply totally confused about their clues. They didn't expect the winner for another hour or so. I was hoping it would either be somebody from our team or Daniel or Jonathan.

I went to the phone booth in the central building and thumbed through the phone book. There were two Frederick Anthonys and an F. Anthony listed. One of them had to be him. How could he look so much like Mr. Carney and not be him? It was too strange.

I was getting a can of pop when Jimmy Fritz spotted me and jogged over. "Toby! Did you win?"

"I've got to talk to you," I said, and we sat while I told him the whole story.

"So you quit is what you're basically telling me, right?"

I nodded miserably. "I know the story doesn't sound like much, but—"

"It sure doesn't."

"But I'm a junior deputy, and I investigate stuff. You have to admit this is a real puzzle."

"Yeah, but who cares? You had a job to do, an assignment, and you didn't do it. You let down your teammates, and you let me down. We can't win now, with you not even finishing."

"I know. I'm sorry."

"You should be, Toby. It's like you just got distracted. If there was an emergency, fine. If there was some crime, sure, you stop to tell someone. But you see a stranger who looks like someone you hardly know, and you make a big case of it? That doesn't wash."

"I know." It hurt like everything to have disappointed Jimmy. I looked at the ground.

"Let me tell you a story," he said, "from my first year at college. I was in a class called Personal Evangelism. You know what that is?"

"Telling people about Christ?"

"Exactly. You memorize verses, and you train. You practice on each other, and sometimes you go out and just talk to people about God on the streets."

"Uh-huh."

"Well, one day on my way to class I saw a homeless man out on the road near the campus. I think he was hitchhiking. I felt sorry for him, and even though I knew he would probably ask for money and use it for booze if I gave him any, I decided to go out and talk to him.

"He was pretty drunk, and I don't know how much he understood. He wasn't ready to receive Christ right then, but it seemed to me I was getting through to him. I made him promise he would at least think about what I said and go to a church or a mission to get more information. He said he would, even though I didn't give him any money."

"That's neat."

"Well, I thought so too," Jimmy said. "Until I got to class. Our professor, a crusty old guy who had been there forever, sort of enjoyed embarrassing people in front of the class."

"That's no good."

"Maybe not, and I would never do it. But he felt I deserved it, so he gave it to me."

"What did he say?"

"He said, 'Mr. Fritz, it's nice you could join us today, thirty minutes late.'

"I said, 'I'm sorry, sir, but I have a good excuse.'

"He said, 'Oh, I'd love to hear it. I'm sure we all would.'

"I said, 'Well, sir, I was doing what you've been teaching us to do in this class. I was witnessing to a homeless man on the street.'

"'Oh, you were?' he said.

"I nodded. Toby, I had good motives for talking to the homeless man, and I cared about his soul, but frankly I was a bit proud of myself. You know what that professor said? He said, 'Mr. Fritz, don't you think God knows your schedule?'

"I said, 'My schedule? Sure, He knows my schedule.'

"And the prof said, 'God knew, even if you didn't, that you had a commitment this morning. You had a responsibility to be in this classroom at the appointed time.'

"Well, he was clearly looking for an apology, but I was kind of defensive. I said, 'Don't you think God cared about that man and gave me the words to say to him?'

"And the prof said, 'Don't you think God can save that man with or without you?'

"I was pretty upset about that for a while, thinking that the professor was more worried about his class than about saving souls. And for sure he was harder on me than he needed to be, and like I say, I would never embarrass someone in front of a class that way. But he was right. It was OK for me to care about that homeless man and his soul, but it would have also been the right thing for me to pray for him while getting to class on time."

"So," I said, "are you saying that it's never right to do anything that isn't on your schedule?"

"Not necessarily," Jimmy said. "As I said, in some emergency cases—like if that man had been staggering in the middle of the road, about to be hit by a car, I would have been right in rescuing him. And if the man you thought you recognized today was doing something illegal or dangerous, it might have been right for you to check him out."

I was feeling pretty stupid. "Will you forgive me?" I said.

"Of course," he said, "but I think you owe an apology to the rest of the team."

"But we already won the overall team competition. This didn't mean that much."

"Don't get me started on that," Jimmy said.

And I could tell he was exasperated with me. I knew I was wrong. "I didn't mean it that way," I said. "I just meant—"

"You just meant that if we still had a chance to lose, you would have stayed focused on what you were supposed to be doing."

"Yeah, I guess that's what I'm saying. But what if I find out that this guy really is Max Carney and that he's lying about being somebody else?"

"What if he is? I'd be thrilled for you if you expose some bad thing and make it right, but even if that happens, it doesn't justify what you did today. You let—"

"I know. I let everybody down."

"I'll want you to talk to the team when they get back. And then we can put this behind us."

"We can? Because you've made me feel awful."

"*I've* made you feel awful? I think you should take responsibility for your own actions, don't you?"

"OK, but I still feel awful."

"Because you were wrong or because you think I'm disappointed in you?"

"Both."

"Well, you've already got my forgiveness, and tonight you'll have the team's. Then if you still feel awful, there may be Someone else you need to talk to about this. You know who I'm talking about?"

"Of course."

Facing the Guys

Neither Jonathan nor Daniel finished in the top ten, but Daniel's team won the scavenger race. Was he excited! He flashed his medal around and wore it on his neck until bedtime. I knew he would wear it home the next day, especially with his dad picking us up.

It was sort of fun watching the medals being passed out and hearing all the stories of mix-ups and mistakes. But I also dreaded having to face my team. They all wanted to know why we didn't even place. The rumor got around that I would be explaining it later, which I had to do. The way I felt, though, I knew it would take more than admitting my mistake to my team to settle the thing.

I prayed about it privately. I knew there was something to the mystery, and I was going to keep checking it out somehow, but I prayed for forgiveness for being irresponsible. I didn't know how else I could have tried to figure out who Max Carney's double was, but I should have come up with something.

Our team met in our cabin. I almost cried as I tried to explain.

Jimmy had told me that confessions and apologies have to be unconditional. "Don't say, 'I'm sorry, but—'" Jimmy said. "If you're sorry, you're sorry, and if you were wrong, you were wrong. There may be reasons, but there aren't excuses. If you want to say what you were doing and why you wrongly thought it was the right thing to do, fine. But the point is to admit you were wrong and take responsibility for your own actions."

And so I did that.

The guys were good about it, and some of them wanted to know more about the mystery and about my little club called the Kalamazoo County Junior Deputies. Jimmy told me it was OK to tell the guys about that stuff but not while I was apologizing.

Of course, we still won the overall championship, and everybody decided that bike camp had been a great way to spend a week.

On the way home Jonathan and Daniel and I spent most of the time sleeping. But when I finally had time to tell them my story, even Mr. Jackson was interested.

"You know," he said, "your dad has the job I want. I'd love to be some sort of a deputy or a detective."

"It *is* fun," I said.

Jonathan, the redhead, leaned forward from the backseat. "You wanna be a Junior Deputy, Mr. Jackson?" he asked. "We might be able to make a special exception for somebody older'n twelve!"

Mr. Jackson laughed that huge laugh of his, but then he became serious. "Really, Toby," he said. "What are you going to do?"

"I don't know," I said. "I want to talk to Thomas and see what he knows about where Mr. Carney goes on weekends. Then I'm going to volunteer to help my cousin with his paper route in the park area where Mr. Carney lives. There have to be some clues there. I want to see him up close again too. If those are really two different guys, I want them to meet each other."

My dad was not as excited about this case as the Junior Deputies were. "There is nothing wrong with looking like someone else," he said. "In fact, there's nothing wrong with pretending to *be* someone else if you're not committing a crime."

"Really?" I said. "If that's really Max Carney from Lake Farm pretending to be Fred Anthony in Muskegon on weekends, there's nothing wrong with it?"

"It's a little weird, I'll admit," Dad said. "But unless he's defrauding an employer or a wife, it's his life."

"What does defrauding mean?"

"Fraud is a lie. The law says it's deliberate deception, fooling someone on purpose in order to benefit financially. In other words, lying to make money."

"Dad," I said, "I know I'm new at this, but I can't figure out why Mr. Carney would do this unless he was doing something wrong."

"So check it out," Dad said. "Prove to me that Max Carney and Fred Anthony are the same person, and I'll work with Muskegon authorities to find out what he's up to. You know you can't confront him or accuse him of anything. You kids just use your powers of observation, look closely and see if there's some way to tell whether this is one person or two, and bring me evidence. OK?"

I was excited, and so were the other Junior Deputies. We started on Sunday, when we were all in church together, asking Thomas if he knew of any unusual things about Max Carney that wouldn't be true of Fred Anthony if they were two different people.

"What do you mean, unusual things?" Thomas said. "I try not to look at him too much."

"Well, you have to do that now," we told him. "Does he have a scar or a bruise or is he missing a finger?"

"I don't know. I don't think so. But I've got some questions for your dad at Sunday dinner."

At our house a couple of hours later, Thomas asked Dad if there were any physical things that were like fingerprints but that could be seen by anyone.

"Good question," my dad said. "One thing that stays the same from baby pictures through adulthood is your ears." He showed us pictures of Kate and me as babies, and we all studied how our ears looked soon after we were born. The ears were smaller, of course, but they had the same shape and skin folds, and they stuck out at the same angles.

"The other thing to look for," Dad said, "is hands. Hands do look a lot alike among brothers and fathers and sons. But if Carney and Anthony are two different people, it should be only their faces that look similar. If their hands are identical too, it's very unlikely you're looking at two different people, especially two who are not related."

Daniel and Jonathan and Joel had never seen Max Carney and didn't have any plans to visit Lake Farm soon. So their role in this case was just going to be reacting to what we found out and giving their opinions. Of course, my parents didn't want Kate having anything to do with a mysterious man, and she didn't seem interested in the case anyway.

So the main work would fall to Thomas and me.

Thomas had no idea what Max Carney did when he left Lake Farm after working Sunday through Thursday nights. "I never thought about it or cared," he said. "I learned to just stay out of Max's way. The best way to get along with him is to not cross him."

My older cousin Steve said I could help him deliver papers Monday after school. He said he had the Carneys on his route and that he often saw Mr. Carney in the afternoon, getting ready to go to work.

"I've never talked to him much," he said, "and his wife always pays the bill."

The plan was that I would try to get a good look at Mr. Carney Monday afternoon and that Thomas would then pay more attention than usual that evening. The next day we would compare notes and see if we could come up with one or two things that would not likely be identical in a person who just looked like Carney in the face. If we could come up with something, then we might be able to talk my dad into taking us to Muskegon the next weekend to see if we could get another look at the so-called Fred Anthony.

The next afternoon my cousin pointed out the Carney house and told me when Mr. Carney usually left for work. I walked around the corner and stalled a little at the house next door until I heard him coming out of the house through the garage to his car.

I shifted the newspaper bag to my other shoulder and walked quickly up his walk. "Well, hi, Mr. Carney!" I said as brightly as I could.

I was amazed at how friendly he was. "Oh, hi, there!" he said. "Thomas Christian's friend, isn't it?"

"Yes," I said.

"Toby?"

I nodded.

"I forget the last name."

"Andrews."

"Sure. How are you?"

"Fine. Um, Mr. Carney, you know, I was in Muskegon Saturday, and I saw a man who looks exactly like you. Exactly."

"Is that so? Who was it?"

"He said his name was Fred Anthony. He was golfing."

"Well, that's one thing we wouldn't have in common," Mr. Carney said. "I've never golfed."

I was so surprised at his friendliness and calm answers

that I forgot to look closely at his hands or his ears. He said he had to get going, so I said good-bye and immediately started to wonder if I was crazy. Two men looked alike, that's all. Neither had heard of the other.

Even if I *was* wrong, and even though Mr. Anthony seemed meaner than Mr. Carney—at least the one I had just talked to—I still wanted them to meet each other. That would be something to see.

Lucky for me, Thomas was more alert that night when Max Carney came on duty. Thomas found a reason to talk to him a couple of times during homework period and again just before lights out. The next day in school, he told me what he had noticed.

"I memorized what his hands look like," he said. "I can't tell you how they're any different than anyone else's. I mean, he's got a thumb and four fingers on each hand, hair on his knuckles, and his nails were plain."

"Plain?"

"He doesn't bite them, they aren't split, he has no purple nails from hitting them with a hammer or getting them caught in a car door or something. But I'd know those hands if I saw 'em again."

"How would you be able to tell his hands from anyone else's, let alone Fred Anthony's?" I asked.

"I just memorized them, that's all. If your dad is right, and no two people—unless they're related—have hands that look the same, I should be able to tell. I also looked at his ears."

"What about them?"

"They're normal, I guess, except his earlobes are not attached. You know what I mean?"

"No."

"Well, like yours and mine are attached to the sides of our heads. They don't hang down. His do hang down a little. And the earlobe on his left ear has a little crease in it."

"Wow, Thomas, you really *are* a detective!"

Thomas smiled and looked down. "Well, we try," he said, pretending to be humble.

I smacked him on the arm. When he glared at me, I remembered how much bigger and stronger he was, and I must have looked scared.

He burst out laughing.

That night my dad said he wasn't excited about wasting a weekend day driving all the way to Muskegon, but there was no other way to see if Anthony was Carney. I think he could see how excited we were, and my mother said something about how both Thomas and I needed some time with just Dad.

Next Saturday morning we got up early and drove to Lake Farm, where my dad signed Thomas out for the rest of the weekend, promising to bring him back after Sunday dinner as usual.

"You're not taking him out of state today or tomorrow, are you?" the woman at the front desk asked.

"No, ma'am," Dad said.

As soon as we were out of the driveway, we headed for the expressway and Muskegon.

Dad told us that if the man I saw on the golf course was actually Carney, he probably wouldn't risk playing at the same place two Saturdays in a row. "If he's there, he's probably just a look-alike. Unless he just doesn't think *you* would show up two weeks in a row."

Dad also said that he himself would stay out of sight, just in case I was right. "If Anthony is really Carney, he'll know we've exposed him if he sees me. Then he might run before we can figure out why he's doing this."

"Then I would spook him too, wouldn't I?" Thomas said.

"Yes," Dad said. "But you're the one who knows exactly what those ears and hands look like on Max Carney. We're going to have to get you into a position where you can see him and he can't see you."

"Close enough where I can see those kinds of little things?"

"Yeah. It won't be easy."

"It seems I will be just as threatening to him," I said. "I mean, him seeing me two Saturdays in a row."

"True," Dad said, "and he has to remember what he said to you as Fred Anthony, and he can't look too shaken, or he'll give himself away. Of course, we're assuming this is Carney pretending to be Anthony. We may be totally wrong."

Both Thomas and I said we knew that, but as soon as we pulled into the parking lot at the private country club in Muskegon where Fred Anthony played golf, I knew we were right.

"Dad," I said slowly, "that's the car I saw in Max Carney's driveway Monday afternoon."

"Are you sure?"

"He's right," Thomas said. "That's Max's car. He drives it to Lake Farm every afternoon."

"That's really all we need to know," Dad said.

"But we want to make sure," I said.

"Me too," Thomas said. "Let's do this."

The Ride

Dad slowly cruised past Max Carney's car and wrote down the make, model, and license number. Then he looked around carefully to be sure no one would see him and become suspicious. He got out of the car and peered through the front window of Carney's car and wrote down the Vehicle Identification Number embedded in the dashboard.

Then Dad drove to the far end of the lot and parked where no one could easily see him. The place was not nearly as crowded as it had been the week before during the tournament. We were under a big shade tree, where we sat and talked about strategy.

Dad had assignments for each of us and said that, while we were carrying them out, he would get to a phone and check on Carney's car. "I'll also talk to the police here in Muskegon if anything comes up fishy on the state computer."

It was more important for Thomas to stay out of sight than for me. I was going to try to meet and talk with Carney again, see if I could rattle him, shake him a little. Thomas was going to try to find a spot where he could eventually see Carney without Carney seeing him.

Thomas waited outside on a bench in the shade. If he happened to see Mr. Carney, he would move out of sight. I went into the pro shop first and bought three new golf balls. Then I went into the clubhouse and asked the man at the desk if Mr. Anthony had already begun his round of golf.

He checked his log on a clipboard. "Yes. Teed off about an hour ago. He's in a threesome, so they should be making pretty good time."

"I need to take these to him," I said, showing the golf balls. "Where do you think he'd be about now?"

Dad had told me not to lie, not to say Mr. Carney had asked for the balls or told me to bring them. "Just say enough that the man can think what he wants," Dad said.

"He's probably still on the front nine," the man said, "but he won't be far from the turn. I'll buzz Ben and tell him to let you borrow a cart. Just stay clear of players and head straight to nine. If he's close, you'll see him. And then you bring that cart right back, you hear?"

"Yes, sir," I said.

I ducked out to tell Thomas what I was doing and to let him know he didn't have to worry about Mr. Carney walking past for a while. We scouted around for a few minutes and found a phone booth off to the side on the way from the course to the outdoor lounge and the locker room.

I would watch for the Fred Anthony threesome at the end of their round and tell Thomas when to take his place in the phone booth. If he stood the right way, he would have his back to Mr. Carney when he walked by, be able to see the man in the reflection of the glass, and then turn to get a close look at his profile, his left ear, and his hands as he passed.

Thomas went back out to the parking lot to wait for my dad to get back from whatever phone he had found. I told Thomas he had probably a little more than an hour before he had to come back and get into the phone booth.

I headed for the golf cart corral, where the old man named Ben had already been tipped off by the man at the counter that I was coming. "You're the young fella who's gonna run some golf balls out to Mr. Anthony, is that it?"

"Right," I said.

"Take number 27 over there," he said. "I assume you've driven one of these before."

"Well, I—"

"There's nothin' to it. Just put the key in, turn it, when the engine comes on, put the switch in Forward, and step on the pedal easy. Don't speed, watch out for people, and bring it straight back here. OK?"

I said, "OK," but the only cart I had ever driven was a go-cart, where all you did was hit the gas or the brake. He gave me the key—on a big leather strap—to a cart that was located right between two others in a long row of carts. I wouldn't be able to turn right or left until I pulled away from the carts on each side. I wasn't quite sure how to get into the thing, since there was no space on either side. I could get into the cart at the end of the line and walk through all of them until I got to mine. But that seemed stupid. I wondered why he hadn't just given me a cart on the end.

I'm sure nobody was watching, but as I climbed into the cart from the back, it seemed as if everybody was. Surely there was a better way to get in. Even getting in from the front would have been easier. I got hung up trying to crawl over the bag holder, and my foot was stuck under one of the struts. Unfortunately, my weight was going forward.

I hoped my foot would just slip out as I sat down, but it didn't. I don't know how I kept from pulling my hip out of joint, but when I flopped from the back into the big seat, my foot was still caught behind me, and my leg was over my head.

Now, when I sort of wished someone *had* noticed and

could help me, I was on my own. Even Ben was talking with some golfers who were turning in their carts. I tried to lurch up and then down and then sideways. Finally I had to roll almost onto my side and kick a few times before my foot came loose. But that was only because my shoe came flying off and bounced onto a seat three carts away.

Now I had to crawl through those carts to find my shoe. When I found it, I sat in that cramped little area trying to put it on, and I leaned onto the horn. *Oogah.*

Everybody, including Ben, looked.

I smiled sheepishly, and he waved and hollered at me.

"That's not twenty-seven!" he shouted. "Three carts over!"

I nodded my thanks and edged my way through the carts back to my own and settled behind the wheel. Ben turned back to his customers, and I tried to remember what he had told me. The little gear switch had to be in Forward. I reached down and yanked it out of Neutral and into Forward.

Then I tried to put the key in, but I had it upside down. I didn't even realize that until I couldn't get it to slide all the way in. Meanwhile, two other cart drivers had come and jumped into their carts and pulled away.

I finally got the key in straight, put my left hand on the steering wheel and my right on the key, and turned it on. I had forgotten that I wasn't supposed to have the cart in gear until after I had turned it on. It jumped forward, which surprised me and made me yank on the wheel. The cart immediately turned left and hooked the cart next to it.

I tried to jam on the brake, but hit the accelerator instead, and my cart rolled up over the wheel of the one next to me, my back bumper caught its front bumper, and I almost flipped my cart over as I bounced and clanged away from the others, pulling one out of line before I broke free.

I felt a hundred eyes on me. I froze, my foot all the way to the floor on the gas pedal, both hands finally on the wheel trying to straighten the thing out, wondering who was going to clean up the mess behind me.

A little crushed-stone drive led from the cart corral to a path to the first tee. Of course, cart drivers were expected to drive slowly and carefully, because that drive went through an area where people loaded their bags, and then it led onto the grass through an opening in a wood fence that was just barely wide enough for one cart.

Well, I flew, and people jumped out of the way. An old woman had her club bag on a two-wheeled hand cart, which I ran over, and she screamed and skipped away. I hollered, "Sorry!" as I shot toward that small opening in the fence.

When I was within a few feet of it I knew I wasn't lined up right, and I still hadn't thought to take my foot off the gas. If I had been able to slow down or even hit the brake, I would have been able to straighten out the cart and go through the opening easily. But now I was scared and embarrassed and hanging on for dear life.

At the last instant, just before I rammed into the left side of the opening, I leaned hard to the right and yanked on the steering wheel, which sent the cart up on its two right wheels. I flew through the opening on two wheels and was about to roll all the way over when the back left tire hit the fence and knocked me back down.

I bounced in the seat, still with the gas pedal to the floor, and my weight made me pull the steering wheel to the left. I kept straightening the cart by yanking right and then left, weaving down the fairway, a long way from the path.

Finally I was in an open stretch, probably where I wasn't supposed to be, but that gave me time to calm down, straighten out, and pull my foot off the gas. I slowed enough to finally be in control of the cart. I looked for the way to the ninth hole, then glanced over my shoulder to see what I had left behind.

People were pointing, helping the old lady, looking at the

fence. I was sorry and hoped I wouldn't be in trouble when I got back, but I couldn't worry about that now. When I turned back around, I was five feet from a small tree. I flew around it, but now I was heading for a clump of bigger trees.

This time I knew enough to hit the brake, but I had never realized how light those carts were. I jammed on the brake, expecting to gradually slow or skid to a stop, but the thing just stopped dead, and I went flying headfirst over the steering wheel.

Somehow, on my way up, my foot caught the gear lever and pulled it out of Forward, past Neutral, and into Reverse. As my thighs banged off the steering wheel, it rotated to the left. I wound up on the ground, dazed, sitting in front of a big tree, glad I wasn't hurt worse.

But now the cart, in Reverse and with the wheels turned all the way left, was coming at me. I rolled, and it just missed me and the tree. I jumped up and tried to grab it, but all I did was straighten it out.

Fortunately, it was not rolling fast, so there I was, chasing that backwards cart as it rolled back to the grassy area. When I was finally able to jump in, I should have just stepped on the brake again, but I reached down and pulled the gear lever back into Forward. The cart stopped and jerked the other way, throwing my head back.

Finally I hit the brake and collected myself. I think I had finally been through everything the cart could throw at me, and now I was ready to drive it. I looked to see exactly where I was, got on the cart path, and drove carefully toward the ninth hole.

By the time I got out of sight of the people at the cart corral, I was able to pretend I had done this before and that there was nothing to it. But as I got near the ninth hole, I could see Anthony's threesome already leaving the tee at the tenth, and I was off again.

I knew it was wrong to bother golfers until they had

completed a hole, so I followed at a distance as Fred and his two partners played the long tenth. They were all pretty good, from what I could tell. They stayed on the fairway, stayed out of the rough and the sand traps, and all reached the green needing one putt for a par. They all two-putted, except for Fred, who three-putted and then glared at me.

So he had seen me. He was the best golfer of the three of them, but he had had the worst hole. I had bothered him. That didn't concern me. I had a job to do.

I pulled up next to his cart and waited for him to put his putter back into his bag.

He ignored me at first.

"I brought you these," I said, proudly displaying the golf balls.

He squinted and leaned close to see them. "Not my brand or my color," he said. "Thanks, anyway."

"Remember me?" I said.

"Should I?"

"I saw you here last Saturday. I told you you looked just like someone—"

"Yeah, I remember you. I thought you said you didn't live around here. What are you doing here?"

"Looking for you again."

"What now?"

"Well, I talked to the other guy, the one who looks so much like you, and I think he'd like to meet you."

"Yeah? Well, let me tell you something, kid. If he wants to meet me, he'll have to come here. Because I don't care whether I ever see him. Understand? Now bug off."

"Why wouldn't you want to see someone who looked exactly like you?"

"Why would I? What do I care? There's probably lots of guys who look like me."

Somehow I just knew I was talking to the same guy I had seen at Max Carney's house the Monday before. But now he was getting into his cart. I didn't want to wait for Thomas to identify him or my dad to find anything on the computer. I didn't care that his car had already given him away. I just wanted him to admit it.

"C'mon," I said. "You're Max Carney, right? I mean, I know, and you know, so what's the deal?"

He had been pulling away in his cart while his two partners climbed into theirs. He drove up to a hedge and stepped out. He waved to me. "Come here," he said. "Get out of your cart, put it in Reverse to keep it from rolling, turn it off, and come here."

I looked around. It wasn't a secluded or private spot. I wasn't afraid he was going to hurt me. So I did what he said.

As I neared him, he spoke quietly but with great seriousness. "I'm going to tell you this only one more time, and then I don't ever want to see you here again. You got it?"

I nodded.

"You got it?" he repeated. "Because I'm not going to say it twice."

The Dodge

My heart was racing, and I'm sure my face was red. "I don't care," Fred Anthony said, "who you think I look like. Big deal if I have a double. If that's fascinating to him, great. Bring him around and let him peek at me through the fence. He can throw me peanuts if he wants to. But I don't want you coming by here anymore with your stories."

Suddenly I got brave. I knew for sure the man I was talking to was Max Carney, and I said so. "I don't think he looks like you anymore," I said.

"You don't? Well, good. Then get out of here."

"No, I think he *is* you."

"I already told you who I was," he said. "Now beat it."

His partners were calling to him.

"I'll see you at Lake Farm next week when I visit Thomas Christian," I said.

He just shook his head. "You're crazy."

As he and his friends headed for the eleventh tee, I

walked back to my cart, feeling weak in the knees and wondering what Dad would have said if I had gotten Max Carney mad enough to hurt me. When I climbed into my cart, I saw him catch up with his friends and point back at me. Both their carts stopped, and they sat staring at me.

I turned the key, forgetting the cart was in Reverse. It shot backward, making me fall forward onto the horn, and I saw the three men laugh their heads off. As my foot hit the brake, I slammed back again and bounced out of the cart onto the ground.

I got up and dusted myself off, knowing Mr. Carney had done that to me on purpose. He and his friends were still laughing. I had to admit I was going to enjoy it when he got caught doing whatever it was he was doing.

The ride back to the cart corral was a lot smoother than the ride to the tenth hole. Ben came hurrying out to greet me, asking if I wanted him to park the cart for me. I insisted on trying it myself, and except for scraping one of the other carts, I backed it into position fairly well. It seemed to me he was trying to keep from smiling, but he had to act like he was mad because he was in charge of those carts.

I went looking for Thomas to tell him what had happened and to give him an idea as to when he would have to be in position in the phone booth. I found him sitting under the tree where my dad had been parked. I didn't tell him everything about my ride, but he was interested in the grass stains on my jeans.

"There's no doubt in my mind that Anthony is Carney," I said.

"How do you know?"

"He denied it—but remember, I just saw him Monday afternoon. It's the same guy—I don't care what he says."

"Well," Thomas said, "I just saw him Thursday night, and, believe me, I'll know him when I see him."

My dad pulled up with good news. "I talked with the

Muskegon Police Department and the Michigan State Police. That car is licensed and registered to Max Carney of Kalamazoo."

"Then that proves it," I said.

"Not quite," Dad said.

"Why not?"

"We haven't connected Fred Anthony with that car. For all we know, they both might be here."

"Oh, come on, Dad!"

"I know it's unlikely," Dad said, "but so far we have nothing to go on. What if Carney and Anthony *are* two different people, claiming not to be related, or—"

Thomas laughed. "All you're saying is that as soon as the so-called Fred Anthony gets into Max Carney's car, we've got him."

Dad nodded. "You have to assume that if Max Carney spends his weekends here as Fred Anthony, he's got identification papers to prove it. His driver's license, his credit cards, his checkbook, all should be in whatever name he's going by. But that car belongs to Max Carney. So if Fred Anthony gets into it, the law has a right to know whether it's with Max Carney's permission or not."

"And if it's not?" I asked.

"Then we have the right to fingerprint Fred Anthony."

"What will that prove?"

"You never know. He may be pretending to be someone else because he's hiding from the law."

"Then why does he risk using his real name in Kalamazoo?"

"How do we know that's his real name? Maybe his real name *is* Anthony. Maybe it's Carney. Maybe it's neither."

"You think he could have another identity too?"

"Who knows?"

Dad said that Thomas should get into position. "As soon as you know it's him and he passes out of your sight toward the locker room, get back out here to the car and let me know. You and Toby will stay in the car, and I'll move over near his car but out of sight. As soon as he's sitting in that car, I'll identify myself as a sheriff's police officer and make him prove he owns it. If he doesn't, local authorities can take him in."

"But you're not a local authority, Dad," I said. "Can you stop him and talk to him? Does he have to tell you anything?"

"Normally no," Dad admitted. "But based on what I told the Muskegon police, they temporarily deputized me and gave me jurisdiction in this case. I can detain and question him, and then I'm to report to them if I detect any illegal activities."

"Cool."

I asked my dad if I could be somewhere where I could see Thomas when he was watching for Mr. Carney.

"As long as you can't be seen. If he sees you, it could blow the whole deal."

I promised, and Thomas and I went looking for a spot for me. We knew where Thomas would be, and we were less than ten minutes from when he needed to be there. I set up in a little hallway where I could see Fred Anthony and his partners coming off the course and could wave at Thomas so he could have his back to them when they came by.

I sat on a small couch with a newspaper up in front of my face, which I kept lowering to make faces at Thomas, waiting by the phone booth. He was either nervous or didn't think it was funny, because he didn't smile, let alone laugh.

Finally I saw them coming, the three golfers, including the man who called himself Fred Anthony. I waved furiously at Thomas, who ducked into the booth, took the phone off the hook, and turned his back to the men as they came in.

But Fred told his partners to go ahead, that he had to make a call. He seemed patient outside the phone booth for a while, but I could see the tension and fear in Thomas's body.

Thomas was pretending to talk on the phone, but of course he had not placed a call.

After Fred Anthony had stood there several minutes, he tapped on the glass.

Thomas waved at him without turning, and I could see the man was getting mad.

"Come on, son!" he said more than once.

Finally he banged on the door, and Thomas couldn't stall any longer. He quickly hung up and spun to come out of the phone booth, looking down and hiding his face. He hurried past where I was sitting, and I noticed that the man stared after him, looking troubled. He ignored the phone and quickly stepped through the outdoor lounge to the locker room.

Thomas and I sprinted to our car, jumped in, and told my dad the whole story.

"So you never got a good look at him?" Dad asked.

"Not really," Thomas said, breathing hard. "I was going to, but he just stopped and waited, and I had to turn away from him to keep him from seeing my face."

"I think he saw you when you left, though," I said.

"That's what I was afraid of," Thomas said. "I didn't know what else to do. I kept thinking he was going to recognize me."

"I think he did recognize you," I said. "That's why he hurried out. He must know that with the two of us here, someone is onto him."

"But onto him for what?" Dad said. "We still have no evidence of wrongdoing."

"It sure seems like he's running, Dad."

"I know. But will he be dumb enough to run for his car?"

"I hope so," Thomas said. "Then we've got him, right?"

Dad shrugged. "It might be just as well if he asks someone else to drive him somewhere. Then we can dust that car for fingerprints without even having to confront him."

"Dad!" I said quickly. "That guy, right there, the one coming out—he was one of Mr. Carney's partners."

"Really? Let's see where he goes."

The man threw two bags of golf clubs into the trunk of his expensive, late-model car and drove off. As he passed us, Dad followed but kept a distance so it wasn't obvious.

The man turned, heading back to the other side of the clubhouse, and as we stopped at the side of the road, watching, Max Carney slipped out of the locker room and jumped into the car.

"That's the man who told you he wasn't Max Carney?" Dad said with wonder in his voice.

"Yes! He swears he's Fred Anthony."

"That's Max all right," Dad said. "And he's dodging you boys."

"Let's get him, Dad!"

"Can't," Dad said. "There's nothing wrong with a man accepting a ride with his friend, is there?"

"No, but we know who he really is, and he's lying about it."

"Don't forget, we don't know that yet. But I've got an idea."

Thomas and I followed Dad into the clubhouse where he asked the man behind the desk if he could tell him whether Fred Anthony was still on the course. The man checked his clipboard. "Should be in the locker room by now, if not in the lounge. Could very well be gone."

"He should still be here," Dad said. "I'm pretty sure his car is in the lot. Isn't that his car? The black sedan?"

"Let me see," the man said, moving to the door where he could see the lot. "Yup, that's it."

"You're sure?"

"You bet. I've ridden in it a couple of times."

"You're a friend of his?"

"You could say that. Been in his home a few times, met the wife."

"Nice lady, isn't she?" Dad said, guessing.

"The best. You know him?"

"Met him in Kalamazoo."

"Really? Didn't realize he got to Kalamazoo much. His territory is all north."

"His territory?"

"He sells golf equipment. He's got northern Michigan and the Upper Peninsula."

"I didn't know that."

"You can wait for him if you'd like."

"Yeah, we'll wait outside."

We headed out past the phone where Thomas had waited to spot Max Carney.

Dad said, "Let me call the Muskegon police. This is the first I've heard that he has a wife here in town too. That's a crime."

"Two wives? It is?"

"Of course! You know anyone else who has two wives at the same time?"

"No, but is it against the law?"

"It's called bigamy. On suspicion of that alone, and because I saw him with my own eyes and know that man calls himself Max Carney when he's in Kalamazoo, we can have the local authorities dust that car for prints."

The Empty Threat

Dad asked the Muskegon Police Department to dust around the driver's-side door and window quickly and without making a big deal out of it.

"If his prints are there at all, that's where they'll be. This is no murder case, as far as we know, and there's no sense embarrassing the country club."

The police department sent an unmarked squad car that parked right next to Carney's car and lifted prints off the door in just a minute or so.

Meanwhile, Dad took us to the police department, where we used a phone and tape recorder to call the three Anthonys in Muskegon until we found the right one.

Then Dad put me on the phone with instructions as to what to say.

Mrs. Anthony said her husband wasn't home from the golf course yet.

"Could you have him call me at this number when he gets

home?" I said. "I'm Toby Andrews, and I talked to him at the golf course today."

I gave her the number. "Oh, by the way," I said, "I also met your husband in Kalamazoo last week."

"Oh, no, son," she said. "You must be mistaken. Fred has the northern Michigan and U.P. territory for a sporting goods company. He hardly ever gets to Kalamazoo."

"He wasn't there Monday or Thursday then?" I said. "Because I talked to him on Monday, and my friend talked to him on Thursday."

"No, he leaves here on Sundays and doesn't get back until Friday about noon. He spends his whole week up north and has for years."

"Are you sure?"

"Of course. He calls me every night."

"Well, have him call me anyway, OK?"

"Sure."

We didn't have to wait long. The police department had that special line on its own number just for calls like this. It wouldn't be answered at the switchboard, and the number wasn't anything like the police department number. When it rang, my dad signaled me to answer it.

"Toby Andrews?" Max Carney said.

"Yes, hi."

"Where are you?"

"I'm here in town."

"What do you want?"

"I want to know why you have a wife in two different cities. Do you also have kids in each town?"

There was a long silence as the tape recorder rolled.

"How many times do I have to tell you that you're mistaken? A guy looks like me. Why are you making such a big deal out of it?"

"Mr. Carney," I said, "you think that just because I'm a kid I don't know the difference? You think I can't tell that

98

you're the same guy who works at Lake Farm and who's on my cousin's paper route? Just tell me what you're up to, and I'll leave you alone."

On the other end I heard him talking to his wife. "Never mind, honey," he said. "It's just this kid. I'll get rid of him. Just never mind."

He waited, obviously until she was out of the room again, and then he hissed into the phone. "Now you listen to me. I'm not admitting anything or telling you anything. But I am warning you. You leave this alone. Just leave this alone. There are things you don't know and could never understand, so just keep your nose out of it. It's bigger than you are and none of your business."

"It's my business if you're working at a Home where my friend lives and you have a secret nobody knows."

"Was your friend here today too?"

"Why?"

"Because I saw him. I don't know who's with you guys, but you'd better get out of Muskegon and leave me alone, and don't even raise the subject next time you think you see me in Kalamazoo."

"How did you know it was my friend if you've never heard of Lake Farm?"

"Just leave it alone," he repeated. And he hung up.

"Should we keep the pressure on, flush him out, have Toby call him again?" Dad asked the detective running the tape machine.

But before he could answer, a cadet brought in a message. The fingerprints had been run through the state and federal agencies and had come up with a match. We all gathered around the table as the name was revealed and the criminal file was opened.

A man named Anthony Maxwell had a record of marrying women and then taking all their money before disappearing. He never divorced them and had a string of at least eight

99

marriages in the Eastern states from more than ten years before. He had been convicted of bigamy three times and had spent several years in prison. The picture in the file was of the man I had talked to on the golf course that day.

The law enforcement agencies had lost track of him, and now it looked like he had settled down in the Midwest. He wasn't stealing money from women and disappearing anymore, but what we had found made it look like he was still trying to keep up with two marriages at the same time.

"Any outstanding warrants?" Dad asked.

The detective nodded. "Interstate flight to avoid prosecution about eleven years ago. He disappeared. He'd been charged with fleecing a woman out of her life savings. I guess he was a real charmer back then."

"He sure isn't very charming now," I said.

"To some people he is," the detective said. "The people at the country club sure like him. I guess he's generous and friendly."

"And he's out of town a lot," Dad said with a smile. "That makes for a good friend."

"I even knew of the guy," the detective said. "He's involved in a lot of civic activities. I never would have guessed. This is a good collar, Deputy Andrews."

"Thanks," Dad said, "but this collar belongs to Deputies Andrews and Christian, these two characters." He pointed at us.

"You want to have some fun?" the detective said. "That is, if it's all right with your superior officer."

Dad nodded. "Within reason," he said.

"We can use them as decoys one more time. We'll make sure they're not in danger, but they can help us get him away from his house so the arrest will be easier. We don't like to have to go in and cuff a guy in front of his wife and kids. And sometimes guys in that situation do something stupid like trying to take hostages or threatening someone. Sometimes they try to run, and that just makes everybody's job harder."

"What's your idea?" Dad asked.

"We'd set up squads down the street from his place, out of sight but where he'd have to come through us if he went anywhere. Then we'd have the boys call him and hint that they know more than he would ever dream they could. They could offer to meet with him, maybe offer a way he can get them to leave him alone."

"I like it," Dad said. "Of course, he's not going to agree to meet with kids, but this should make him run. But what is he going to use for wheels—his wife's car?"

The detective laughed. "I wonder how he explained that one to her, coming home without his car. Well, they certainly have two vehicles. We're going to impound the one at the country club. He'll have to use his wife's to go out at all."

"He's going to wonder how these kids got to Muskegon, and he's got to figure they've got a parent or some other adult with them," my dad said.

"If he's thinking straight, maybe," the detective said. "Right now he's got to be so spooked he doesn't know whether he's coming or going. If he asks, the kids can say you brought them but that you won't be with them at the meeting place."

"That'll be true, because they won't be there either, right?" Dad said.

"Exactly."

"Let's do it."

The detective said he thought it would work best if Thomas and I went with the police while they set up the stakeout a couple of blocks from Anthony Maxwell's house. Then we could call him from a squad car on a cellular phone. It seemed so strange to call him Anthony Maxwell, because I had always known him as either Max Carney or Fred Anthony.

And it was weird to think that neither of Maxwell's wives

knew about the other. I wondered what the one in Kalamazoo thought he was doing every weekend. Maybe he used the same story on her: that he was a golf equipment salesman in northern Michigan for a sporting goods company.

The Muskegon detective agreed that my dad could be in another car so I would be able to truthfully say he wasn't with us. "But why are you so worried about telling the truth to a criminal?" the detective asked.

"We teach our kids to always tell the truth," Dad said. "I don't have a problem with misleading a bad guy once in a while when I know I'm protecting people from him. But there's no need for a twelve-year-old to get into the practice of lying, regardless of the reason."

"I respect that," the detective said. "We'll set it up so the boys can be as straightforward as possible."

Dad was with some uniformed officers in another squad car while Thomas and I sat in the backseat of the detective's car.

"Your dad has quite a reputation around the state," he told me. "Did you know that?"

"Well, I know he wins a lot of the pistol matches."

"Oh, everybody knows that," the detective said. "But he's considered a cop's cop. The kind of a guy you'd like with you when your life is on the line. Does everything by the book, does it right, and has great instincts. You want to be a sheriff's deputy when you grow up?"

I shrugged. "I don't know. I like all this stuff, but I guess it's too early to decide."

"How about you?" the detective asked Thomas.

"I don't know if I want to be a cop or not," Thomas said, "but I'd sure like to be like Mr. Andrews."

"I agree, son. You can't do better than that."

That made me wish I'd said what Thomas said. I knew he liked and respected my dad, but I didn't know he felt that strongly about him. It shouldn't have surprised me. I never wanted to take for granted that I had a dad that people wanted to be like. I wanted to be like him too. That's one of the reasons it was cool to be a junior deputy.

It was dark by the time we got into position. Then the detective put Thomas and me on cellular phones so we could both listen and talk at the same time. The detective thought the call should come from Thomas this time. That, he said, would really get Maxwell's attention.

Thomas asked for Max Carney. The wife said there was no one there by that name. "Well, would you just tell your husband that Thomas Christian is asking for Max Carney?"

"I hate to bother him," she said. "We're about to go and pick up his car, which he lent to a friend."

"Just tell him that, ma'am. If he won't talk to me, I'll understand."

We could hear her giving her husband the message.

He said, "Give me that phone and give me some privacy. I'll get rid of these pranksters once and for all." He took the phone, and after we heard a door shut, he finally spoke. "Hello, who is this?"

"Thomas."

"Thomas, what do you want?"

"I just wondered if you wanted to know how much we know about you, Mr. Carney? Or is it Mr. Anthony? Or is it Mr. Maxwell?"

"Listen, Christian, you know I can make things tough for you. Whatever you think you know, you keep your mouth shut about it, you hear?"

"We might," I broke in.

"You again," he snapped. "You're behind this whole thing. You don't know who you're dealing with."

"No, you don't know who *you're* dealing with," I said, and that was sure the truth.

"We might be persuaded to shut up," Thomas said. "Why don't we get together and talk about it?"

"Who's with you?" Maxwell asked.

"Why?"

"How'd you get here?"

"My dad brought us," I said.

"Where's he?"

"He's not with us now, and he won't be with us if you meet with us."

"What's in it for me?"

"Just the chance to shut us up."

Maxwell was silent for a moment. "Where?" he said finally.

We told him about a convenience store about a mile from the country club. He said he'd meet us there.

But the detective agreed with my dad and said Maxwell was too smart for that. "He doesn't trust you and has no reason to. He has to be convinced you have told your father, and even if he doesn't know your dad's a cop, he wants nothing to do with people who know. I say he'll make a run for it."

The detective was right. When Mr. Maxwell came out of his house, his wife was not with him. Yet he had two large suitcases and a box. He loaded her car and took off in the opposite direction from the country club, heading north.

He was pulled over by the Muskegon police, and his whole phony life fell apart. He's in prison now, and his families in Muskegon and Kalamazoo were shocked and embarrassed.

Once again the Junior Deputies got a lot of credit in the newspaper and on the news. That was only good for our business. We wanted more cases. They didn't all have to be this famous or mysterious.

But Thomas and I decided on the way back home that

night that if it weren't for having to go to school every day, we'd have pretty cool lives.

"Too bad only the adults get paid for this kind of work," he said.

I laughed, and we both curled up and tried to sleep. It wasn't easy. I was still excited about how much we'd been allowed to do on the case. And I was proud that my dad had such a good reputation, with kids and adults.